THE CONQUEST OF THE PLANETS

By
JOHN W. CAMPBELL, JR.

I0541428

ARMCHAIR FICTION
PO Box 4369, Medford, Oregon 97504

COULD EARTH RETURN TO ITS FORMER GREATNESS?

Mankind on Earth had fallen into a state of physical and moral decay, so much so that the human colonists on all the other planets of the Solar System cut ties with their mother world. Hundreds of years later, though, a rejuvenation of humanity was starting to take place on Earth. It started deep inside a deserted underground city where a young boy, Bruce Lawry, discovered a crumbling, ancient building—a library, with rows of books filled with the knowledge of Earth's past greatness. As the years went by, Bruce and his followers slowly regained the knowledge it would take for mankind to raise itself to the heights of greatness once again. But one thing stood in the way—the decadent despots that ruled Earth's cities. They had long ago sentenced most of mankind to a life of slavery in cities carved out beneath the surface. But now, armed with new science and new weaponry, the people of Earth's underworld were ready to fight for their freedom.

FOR A SECOND COMPLETE NOVEL, TURN TO PAGE 131

CAST OF CHARACTERS

BRUCE LAWRY
As a young boy he crawled through the darkness of a deserted city—and what he found there helped change the world.

DON WADE
There was no one on Earth who knew more about Earth history, including the rise and fall of mankind, than Don Wade.

JOHN MONTGOMMERY
Some people felt he was a self-serving, arrogant politician, but the decision he made would someday save the Earth.

LORA WAYNE
She was loyal, steady, and brilliant—and she was terribly in love with the most important man on Earth.

OMALLIN
A cockroach among tyrants. His lust for power was nearly equaled by his overindulgent lust for any attractive woman.

PHILIP LAURIE
His brilliance helped man reach out to the distant planets—but his methods came close to destroying the culture of Earth itself.

DOT STEEL
She was one of the first to see the amazing discovery within the forgotten cube, but would she live long enough to tell about it?

PROLOGUE

THE crowded men, a full hundred and twelve cramped in a tiny concrete room, were unbelievably quiet and tense. Only one small light, thrown on the tuning controls of the big set, relieved the absolute darkness that seemed to push in from the windows. McLaughlin, at the controls, was quietest of all. His ears were intensely aware of the strange rushing roar, like heavy ocean surf, that beat out through the loudspeaker.

A voice struggled through the washing sound. "Elevation about twenty-five miles now. Incredibly jagged rock. This side much rougher than other. Found a small crater-bottom—we're aiming for that—looks smooth." Again only the washing roar of short-wave static and the tense silence. "Elevation twenty miles. Dropping on rockets. Almost no gravity pull, however. The big boy is pulling us around a bit though. Hard to handle. Tricky motion. Fifteen miles. We've got a horizon now. There is no axial rotation, or we would never make it. Ten miles." Silence. Washing static. "Five miles," the voice reported.

"We've almost stopped—comparatively—now. About a mile and a half to go. Stopped, and falling back. Can you hear the rockets now? They're working fairly loudly. A thousand feet—eight hundred—five hundred—we'll know in a second, and if it's bad—we had a nice time. Try again!"

"We're floating on the rockets. Stevens is doing a wonderful job of it. There's a big pinnacle of rock near us. This floor wasn't so smooth as it looked. We're sinking—we've—" The loud speaker crackled with a tinny, broken rattle, and then only the washing static sounded in it.

A low, heavy groan came from the hundred and twelve men. Three near the door darted out, headed for their offices. The second attempt had failed.

McLaughlin sat just as quietly, and tensely as ever. "They smashed a tube, anyway," he snapped softly. "That doesn't mean they're broken. A tube's a hell of a lot more tender than a man."

The hundred and nine men were rustling and weaving. Listening to the static sounds. "Whatever happened, it happened a long time ago—it takes time even for radio on that hop," someone said. His voice was low, but it seemed a shout in the bare concrete room.

The loudspeaker crackled, hummed and silenced again to washing roar, but an instantaneous quiver ran through the men. "Sorry," said the voice, "probably worried you. Tube gave out. We made a perfect landing, but the slight jar cracked a tube's air-seal."

The rest was lost as a roar went up from the men in the room. A jammed stream squeezed out of the door, like toothpaste from a tube. They squirted out, sprinted for the monorail line near by. Over charred, blackened earth they stumbled and sprawled, cheering.

Five men remained in the room. McLaughlin was talking into his own transmitter now, while the recorder took down every detail of the message coming in from space.

Philip Laurie, the little narrow chested dreamer who had designed the *"Ion,"* was dreaming out loud to big, broad-shouldered John Cummings, the man who had had intelligence and interest enough to listen to the man and his strange ideas.

"It's done, John," said Laurie dreamily. "They've made it."

"They're not on Mars, yet, only Phobos," Cummings replied.

"No difference. Mars is easy now. The little rocket can do it and land with her wings. No trick. They aren't back, either. That's harder. But it doesn't count. To them it does of course, but I mean to Earth. Earth has crossed space. Earthmen have reached another world. That's just the first. In twenty years, John, you will be able to make the trip in a regular, commercial liner-freighter. New colonies! Earthmen colonizing other planets.

"John, that's always been my dream. I can't go—I won't. You gave me control of this. That was my one stipulation. The profits are yours—and there will be profits I promise you—but—" he looked down at himself, and then to the towering, powerful body of his friend. "No more half-men like me. The conditions on those other planets are hard and harder than men ever faced before, and I'm going to set up a control board. There'll be plenty of men willing to go. Look at the thousands on thousands of applications we both got for this trip. But I'm going to combine several of my dreams in this. I'm going to make a greater race of Earthmen, a more powerful, finer, more adventurous race of Earthmen. I hate this body of mine and its weakness. I want all men to have bodies and minds like yours. I will have reason enough to forbid it—and I'm going to forbid the acceptance of one single man or woman who is not physically and mentally perfect.

"Earth is greater this day, and henceforth, she will grow as her children grow!" said Philip Laurie.

It was inevitable. His decision perhaps made it a bit more radical and more rapid, but the result was as inevitable as fate. There were no barbarians to pour in on civilization anymore, but Philip Laurie had cut open Earth's veins, where flowed the richest life-blood of the planet. It was not a greater planet he'd created, not a mightier Earth.

And it was not merely his plan. The very forces that made life harder on those planets would have done it as effectively. Earth's greatness died that day, that hour, it died the very second Robert Gady said, "Sorry, probably worried you. We made a perfect landing."

But the corpse was very large, and it took many centuries for the corruption to spread, and the ultimate decay to destroy it.

*　　*　　*

Bruce Robert Laurie, great grandson of the inventor of the first ship to make the crossing to Mars, was a humble employee in the office of the Interplanetary Transport Examination Service. Bruce Laurie or Tom Jones got the same treatment here. Old Philip Laurie, back in 1983, had fashioned well when he fashioned it. And John Cummings had been willing to trust Laurie. The result had been a board of scientists who had to pass on every man who made that trip, and for four generations that office had been all but flooded, for only an intermittent service was possible. The air ships of that day, even a full century after Laurie's invention, were not free of all troubles. For instance, while they had been able to reach Mars, and the Jovian satellites and the Saturnian satellites, no ship had ever returned from Jupiter's surface. Jupiter's mighty gravity stopped them.

There was much room on those Jovian worlds, and even on Mars, although the colonies were growing swiftly. But there were few ships, and many people trying to go. Interplanetary Transportation had their chance to pick and took it.

Bruce Laurie was hopeful—but fearful. He was twenty-five, just three weeks past the necessary twenty-fifth birthday in fact. He stood five-foot five, rather light in build, but already he had a reputation in engineering.

The girl at the Statistics Desk looked up at him as his turn came.

"Name?" In a moment she had his Vital Statistics card. "Dr. Thomas Drew will see you. Room four-fifty-seven down the hall to the left." Laurie took the card with its series of punched holes on a perfectly blank white card. The indexing machines would read it for Dr. Drew. Laurie entered four-fifty-seven, handed the card to the brisk, pleasant looking doctor, and sat down. The indexing machine had interpreted it for the physician in seconds.

"This is your second visit, is it not, Laurie?"

"Yes, sir. I came immediately after my twenty-fifth birthday."

"Right. The card contains not only all the information you handed in, but of course, much more that we gathered, plus the decision we reached, and why. The decision was against you, I'm sorry to say. You're a fine engineer as your reputation already shows. You have excellent heredity of mental characteristics—but as you know, your famous great-grandfather died of tuberculosis. Your grandfather didn't, probably because we'd conquered the disease by then, but he died at forty-seven of heart disease. Your father died two years ago at fifty-two, of hardening of the arteries, and attendant physical degeneration.

"I'm sorry, Laurie. We need your mentality in the new race we're trying to build up, but your physique isn't designed for hard wear, even here on Earth. I'm not sure you would survive even the space trip. The effects are very severe, due to lack of equalization of blood pressure in the absence of gravitational or other acceleration. If you did survive—your great-grandfather, who of all men had a right to emigrate to Mars, refused to go. You remember when his application automatically came up, he turned it down himself, and he alone voted against it?

"He was right. There is some taint of weakness in your inheritance that has, time after time, robbed the world of powerful minds in their prime. What I have mentioned in connection with your direct descent is equally true of your uncles and granduncles.

"But—go on, Laurie. Your type is needed here on Earth, too. That weakness will be driven out, through the, generations. You may not make the trip, but neither did your great-grandfather. Perhaps your great-grandson will."

Laurie was not greatly surprised as he made his way out of the office and took the moving ways toward the airport for New York once more. But he was vastly disappointed. The moon shone pale in the daylit sky. No Laurie had ever reached even so far.

Some day, he was determined that one of them would. In the meantime, there were still opportunities to make a name for himself here on Earth. Even though there were only two dozen business organizations in the United States, there was room for their ramifications.

*　*　*

Ban Miller had reached that acme of human aims, for the average man of 2243—he had been accepted. Accepted, of course, meant that within two years he would be given a berth in one of the crowded Planetary Transports. Wherefore, since Ban Miller's particular field of mental activity had been news reporting and interpreting, he was now acting as trainer to the Unlicked Cub. The Cub was not wholly unlicked, naturally, but he was inexperienced as far as this field of reporting was concerned. Televiso-news was a highly interesting and effective means of spreading the stories, but the average man did not care to sit before his televisor and watch the International Conference on Planetary Affairs for fifteen all-day sessions, and further, he didn't have the time. The Conference was scheduled to run fifteen days, and the nations were spoiling for a real good battle-royal. It *would* be a battle-royal, too, because the Industrial Committees were fearing a violent depression, and realized that they had the choice of fifteen million unemployed in the United States, and proportionate numbers elsewhere, or a war, which would make the fifteen million and proportionate numbers unproductive consumers in the armies of the world. Further, the war was indicated by falling profits. The customers needed a good reason before they'd accept a price boost. A war would be ideal.

Then incidentally of course, there was real enmity arising from the Planetary Affairs Commissions. For nearly three centuries, the Interplanetary Transportation Company had had practical control and ownership of the planets. Interplanetary had gotten off to such a flying start, it had simply bought up all competition at first, and since then no one had been interested in starting a rival company. The only government of the Planets had been the Interplanetary's own Executive Office. Now however, there had arisen considerable feeling on Earth, that some nation had a definite claim to the control of those planets.

"They'll argue," Miller explained to the Cub, "on the basis of the claims made way back in the late 1900's and the early 2000's. The United States has an iron-clad claim on Mars, really, because it was an all-American crew that took old Laurie's ship up there. But her navigator, and her captain, happened to be of French descent, and France has laws to the effect that no Frenchman can become a national of any other country. Therefore, the captain, when he claimed the planet for the United States had no right to do so, and further, the second ship to make the crossing was actually French, and also claimed half the planet. But Germany pointed out that neither ship had fully explored the planet, and not until their ship made the crossing in 1989 was a complete survey in detail available. Therefore they claim about a third of Mars.

"Now the Jovian Worlds were explored by nationals of all the Terrestrial countries, and Io was explored by an American-born Martian. The big fight of course is over Mars. And—I sort of have a hunch old Terra is in for the shock of her life."

"Why?" asked the Cub.

"Wait and see. We'll know within twenty-four hours."

"Who's that coming in now?" asked the Cub.

"M. Poireau. French Premier. Elected by the Steel interests. He's naturally for war. Steel in France includes aircraft and rockets."

"Who's following him there? I don't recognize him at all."

"Oh—oh! Watch the fireworks! I knew that would happen. Terra is definitely in for a shock. That's John Montgommery, terrestrial president of Interplanetary. 'Mystery Montgommery.' Every time he does show his face, somebody gets blown off the map—look at those delegates there. Every one of them is trembling in his boots right now. Cartwright from 'these United' represents Metals and Allied Utilities, and he's wondering what's up. If he works against Montgommery, he may lose business for Metals—and if he doesn't, why he may lose his job. Metals can have his election 'recounted' any time they want to, and find fraud in it, of course."

"And I, in my innocence, thought there were still some traces of the ancient democratic government left on Earth."

"Funny, lots of people still do. Clerks and so forth think their votes really get counted. Of course, some of the votes do. They may all be counted pretty quickly, though. I hear Metals is going to start taking their employees' fingerprints so they can check up on who voted and how, when they find it necessary."

"The Secret Ballot! What a secret!"

"That gang is worried. All those delegates are worked-up. Montgommery's presence means real trouble. You know they have a true democratic government on the Planets now—something on the order of the old Socialistic schemes proposed here on Earth back in the twentieth century and which Russia even tried out. But what the planets have is supposed to be a corporation-voting idea. Actually—well you'll see, I'm willing to bet. Of course their socialism is a whole lot different from anything they proposed back in the twentieth century. Started that way, you might say, because everything on Mars was owned by Interplanetary to begin with, and every immigrant of course paid his fare by buying 'stock.' But—you'll probably see."

The gentleman from France had been appointed temporary chairman, and so French was the official language of the Conference till the permanent Chairman was elected. He was calling the meeting to order now. The delegates took their places and order ensued. Montgommery had taken a place in the Distinguished Visitors' gallery. More eyes were turned to him than to the Chairman. Montgommery's presence was like the tick of a time bomb. When would it explode?

Sir Reginald Barry of England was made Permanent Chairman according to schedule in rapid-fire order. Almost at once, M. Poireau rose, and in beautiful diplomatic English, beating all around the bush and Robin Rood's barn, stated that France declared one half of Mar's surface area as hers— that half being delineated carefully. It included Mars Center, New Denver, New Berlin, and Salamance. France knew, of course, that the nations would realize the justice of her claims at once, and withdraw any claims of their own. However, France was fully prepared to stand up for her rights—and intended to.

Cartwright of the United States rose, and read his speech. "Notice he's reading a typed speech, and answering all of Poireau's points? That speech of Poireau's was a complete surprise, of course," chuckled Miller. "Now watch Hans Schenkie answer both speeches from his own typed script. Man, this Conference is going to explode in a hurry. Montgommery is the cause of this; they'd have delayed these speeches over a period of days, but they want him to hear their claims. He's taking it all in himself—and they'd just expected a few vice-assistant-seconds to be listening in. Say—hold on here, will you? I want to make a call." Miller rose, and vanished along the corridor.

In perhaps fifteen minutes he was back. Cartwright was answering Poireau's third point by this time, with only eleven more to go. Miller glanced at the Cub's notes and laughed. "Too serious, man, too intent. Here's the way." He condensed the Cub's three pages, to two paragraphs, and explained: "At that rate, you'll fill several large volumes at the average conference, and never be able to find what you wanted again. Those points he's making are all in the Terrestrial Encyclopedia.

"But here's a note to make. The 'New Denver' is due to land tomorrow at noon in New York. But—they've spotted a lifeboat leaving her. The lifeboat broke out five hours ago, and will land in about an hour. I'm waiting. The bomb explodes then. I'll bet it lands right here in Geneva, too."

Cartwright had nearly finished his speech, when the man entered the Distinguished Visitors' Gallery. He was clad in the loose-looking, dust-tight Martian garments, and his face was dark and lean with Martian sunlight. He moved somewhat heavily on earth here, but there was a certain alertness and energy about him. He went directly to John Montgommery, and spoke softly to him. From a briefcase he drew a large envelope of papers, and passed them over with a smile of confidence, and a handshake.

"Ah—it's come. Now, the bomb explodes."

Cartwright had been watching. In remarkable fashion, he concluded his address almost at once. The conclusion was that France's claims were wholly baseless and false according to international law. Mars belonged wholly and singly to the United States of America.

Montgommery rose in his seat.

"Mr. Chairman."

"Mr. Montgommery," acknowledged Sir Reginald. "You have no official status at this meeting, but I am sure we would all be glad to hear your views, as an expert on Martian affairs."

"Mr. Chairman, I should like to present these credentials." Montgommery, dressed in his formal officer's uniform from his earlier years in the military, stalked forward, and passed to Sir Reginald the papers he had just received from the courier.

Sir Reginald looked at them hurriedly, then stopped. He looked again, then smiled slowly at Montgommery. "Surprising, isn't it, how the obvious will escape attention. Gentlemen," he went on, addressing the Conference, "I beg to present Mr. Montgommery, Delegate from the United Planetary Council, and Ambassador Plenipotentiary for Mars. He will explain Mars' answer."

"Thank you, Mr. Chairman," Montgommery replied, interrupting the sudden hushed murmur of surprise and anger. "Gentlemen, I have little to say, but I believe you will agree with Sir Reginald, that it is obvious. Mars does not belong solely and singly to the United States. She does not belong half to France, or one-third to Germany; neither to the Jovian Worlds, nor the Saturnian Worlds. Mars belongs solely and singly to the citizens of Mars.

"The Jovian Worlds belong singly and solely to the colonists of those Jovian Worlds, as the Saturnian Worlds belong to their inhabitants.

"I am, I realize, setting forth a great principle, but it is yet an old principle. It is the principle that set up the United States—that men should determine their own courses of action. We of the Planets desire to do so.

"I fully realize the feelings that will be stirred up, but I intend now in open conference to say, and say bluntly, what we are all thinking.

"Mars, and the Planets, all represent great wealth. Further, they represent room for colonization. Interplanetary has long held absolute control, and only so because of the vast wealth and consumptive power it represented. This very conference represents the culmination of a recent tendency we, who are interested in Planetary affairs, have watched with alarm. Terrestrials want more ships built, more accommodations for interplanetary travel, so that all can move to the Planets who want to, and this pressure of public opinion has gradually been bringing forth legislation that would waken Interplanetary to a point where an undesired rush of colonists would be possible.

"The Planetarians have been carefully selected, and are quite literally a chosen race. The result has been a bit of superiority on their part, but there has always been the opportunity for Terrestrials to be chosen, and this hope has prevented any strong feeling against them.

"But the reason we have given for this selection, so rigorous that we have refused ninety percent of all applicants, has been the limited transportation facilities. Terrestrial governments could build more ships, say the people, and take us there.

"Frankly—Mars doesn't want too heavy an unselected immigration.

"That is the reason for this change, really. Mars is now in theory as well as in fact, a self-governing world. She has been. You all realize that fact, although technically it has been a corporation called Interplanetary Transport. Now the name has been changed to the Martian Planetary Union, a state with powers similar to those of the individual states of the United States of America, in the greater government of the Interplanetary Union.

"We have combined against an undesirable immigration. We need more people, need them badly, and will continue our present system, and expand it—but we will select them. The Interplanetary Union government will appoint as officers the entire staff of the present Interplanetary Transport, renaming them according to the more usual diplomatic practice as Consuls and Ambassadors.

"The immediate reaction on the part of the Terrestrial nations having claims to the Planets will of course be a desire for war. There is a strong economic need for war right now, I understand," Montgommery added bitterly, "but I would like to point out the absurdity of such a course. Mars is not wealthy enough in human and economic capital to desire such a war—but I think it should be remembered that all the existing ships, capable of the Interplanetary crossing, belong solely and exclusively to the newly-created Interplanetary Union.

"Oh, no doubt you could build ships, and attack, within two or three years. What would you gain? You cannot armour a spaceship. They are very tender machines, as we well know. Therefore they could not attack readily, nor effectively. Further, they could not carry fuel for the round trip, and still maneuver. The result would be a fleet of derelict, helpless machines in space, hanging off Mars powerless to move, and completely at the mercy of our own small, swift battle-rockets.

"I believe you will agree that war is out of the question—purely so from a mechanical standpoint. However, I doubt that the people would support such a venture, for they all hope, and secretly expect, to get to Mars themselves. Every man with any self-respect believes himself worthy of choice. Those that feel sure they won't be chosen are cripples, weaklings, or completely spiritless. Of such you cannot make an army. When England tried to put down the rebellion of her American colonies, she failed, not because her men were not brave, or strong or spirited, but because the men of England agreed with their brothers and cousins in the colonies, and refused to fight them. Mercenaries had to be hired, with deplorable results.

"Well—you may find mercenaries. But every worthy citizen of Terra has a real, and genuine chance to join us in the greatest work man has undertaken: the colonization of new worlds by new and better races of mankind."

Montgommery sat down. Suddenly the Cub became aware of the fact that Miller had vanished. In his place was an International Newsman with his televiso projector.

There was an angry mutter of discontent rising from the Conference, and officials were heading for the International Newsman.

"That scene was not directly broadcast of course?" demanded the sergeant-at-arms.

Miller reappeared before the International man could speak. "No, Rafferty, it wasn't. We wouldn't care to put that red-hot stuff on the air. But it's being groomed for broadcast right now. We calmed it temporarily."

"'Fraid it won't go, Miller," said Rafferty, shaking his head. "They all agreed on that. It's bad for the people."

"I'm afraid it has," said a new voice. The messenger from the Interplanetary Union had appeared. "There was nothing we were ashamed to have on the air, and it has all gone out. I have a new ultravisor in the bag here, and it was relayed from my lifeboat. The Conference will have to answer that frank challenge as frankly, if they want the sympathy of the people."

"But don't worry," Miller replied ironically, "those boys will cook up some kind of hash. Or their companies will."

A voice pierced suddenly through the mounting angry buzz from the floor of the Conference. "—all realize that this is the desperate move of a traitorous, jealous German Government to prevent the just claims of France being realized and—" The voice was drowned in a bellow of denunciation from the German Delegate.

"I guess they have already," grinned the Cub. "They've got their war, anyway. I'll send the pictures to you, Miller, if you Martians should be interested."

*　　*　　*

Moon-faced, fat Simon Wallowy was Chairman of the Conference. Simon Wallowy was also Chairman, of the Industrial Committee of the United States of North America, the son of a long line of Wallowys who had been Chairmen of the Committee naturally, because of the vast properties owned by the Wallowy interests.

Simon Wallowy was very much annoyed by this conference, as it had called him away from a very pleasant time he had been having at his country home with a number of Plehb girls he had directed to go there. But—this annoying conference had been necessary. The trouble with the world was that there were a number of semi-Plehbs with a little property, and some influence that could make so much noise, that they influenced opinions adversely. Now if Mortan's idea would just be accepted by some of the other men, this last annoyance could be done away with in another two decades.

However, since things were as they were, the disarmament conference would have to be gone through with. Naturally it would come just when war had almost been decided on by the Sino-Japs and the Americans. Wallowy didn't see what he was going to do with the present unemployment situation, if they didn't have a war fairly soon.

Also he was annoyed by the attitude that John Montgommery had displayed, that annoying attitude of indifferent superiority, as though he was not a descendant of middle-class incompetents, squeezed out of and off Earth by the strife of business. The Planetarians acted as though they had wanted to leave Earth. A billion incompetents and dreamers Earth had gotten rid of, so that a real, stable society could be established, and now these same exiles were 'acting superior.'

They scarcely carried on any trade with Earth anymore, but then Wallowy didn't want it really. He'd have had to make some concessions on the tariffs if he had, and those cheap all-machine-made goods of the Planets would have caused trouble among the workers.

Ah well. Wallowy wandered across the park toward the Conference building. The beautiful, white, silica building, set among the green of trees on the shore of the blue lake, backed by snow-capped mountains, was shimmering pink in the twilight. Above it, a great tongue of azure and golden atomic flame hung motionless and steadies, unmoved by the gentle breeze—the azure and gold of the Peace building.

Wallowy had always been annoyed by it. It reminded him so forcefully of the trouble his grandfather had had when the atomic flames were first invented by David Laurie of Io. The tremendous increase in the available energy had made it possible to throw thousands of workers out, and still maintain production, but it had brought a great deal of trouble, till the British-American war had gotten rid of the excess, and brought Canada into the Union. But it had had the beneficial effect of opening up the Major Planets and Venus and Mercury to colonization, so that a great many of the remaining semi-Plehbs had left Earth, and made things quieter. Anti-gravity had come almost simultaneously, and completely opened the system to colonization, but by that time the Interplanetary Union got nasty, and wouldn't permit any further emigration from Earth.

Wallowy passed through the door of the Peace Palace with a determined waddle. He might be able to induce the Heinrichs and the Derriers to join him in declaring war on the Interplanetary. That would solve the unemployment problem, and might get them a little satisfaction on the score of Interplanetary's superior attitude. He frowned though, as he remembered that Interplanetary wouldn't respect his properties properly. They might cause damage.

An hour later he called the meeting to order. He had intended calling on Karl Heinrich as the first speaker, but he discovered to his annoyance that Montgommery of Interplanetary Union wanted the floor. He ignored him, and called Heinrich to speak.

"I think," said Montgommery interrupting, "that it would be wisest to hear me first. Mr. Chairman, may I have the floor?"

"Very well, Mr. Montgommery. Your manners however, are execrable."

Montgommery smiled slightly, and nodded to him. "Worse, according to your ideas. However, my message has not been heard by you—er—men before." He continued more soberly.

"Interplanetary Union has decided that we have made a bad mistake. Earth, the Mother World, has always, been regarded with some feeling of interest and sympathy. However, we have come more and more to realize that in giving birth to the children, old Earth has been sacrificing her life-blood. I am sadly afraid that the children have been stupid, and selfish. The result is inevitable, of course, but our own interest in our own problems and the vast work that we had to accomplish, in making civilization possible on such bleak worlds as Pluto and Athena, turned our attention from Earth. We have neglected her interests. Now," he smiled, "we have decided that Earth's only hope is that we completely neglect her.

"Interplanetary Union has decided to completely withdraw all relations with Earth. We will withdraw our consuls, ambassadors all our interests. We will send no further ships to Earth. We will send no messenger. We will receive none.

"This should be put on record for future generations. When Earth first sends a ship again to Interplanetary at Mars Center, a new ship, with some new invention of importance, then Interplanetary will revisit Earth, and help her finish settling her problem.

"You do not understand me. Poor Earth has given her life-blood in giving life to the Planets. Earth is nearly dead. We will leave her, for no effort of ours can bring new life to her, only the slow cleansing of Time can do it.

"The planets have, for nearly seven centuries, through thirty generations of men, robbed Earth of her greatest heritage, the near-geniuses. We have accepted only the strong, the intelligent and the healthy. Generation after generation we have taken from Earth everything that makes the human race strong, we have left only the dregs, the weak, the stupid, the unadventurous, and—the contented.

"The result—we can see all too clearly now. Earth still has a remnant of hope—the so-called semi-Plehbs. We know that genius arises slowly, if a thousand morons mate, a few normal men will result. If a thousand normal men mate, a few near-geniuses will result. If a hundred near-geniuses mate, perhaps one genius will rise to lead all the others onward. The planets took every genius Earth produced and nearly every near-genius. They did this not once, but time and time again, through thirty generations. The result was that now nearly all the genes of intelligence and health and wisdom that the human race carried have been isolated on the planets. The genes of stupidity and disease, and every form of weakness have concentrated on Earth. Your death rate shows that, and that, is a benefit. Fortunately, in a machine age, the genes of stupidity lead only to death—sudden and violent death. So, we of the planets have this hope for Earth. Through perhaps another thirty generations, the genes of weakness and disease will kill off their bearers. More and more they will concentrate in certain strains, and bring death.

"Even among your Plehbs there is some opportunity for intelligence, there will be such a divisioning that the more intelligent will be thrown together, and there will slowly rise a group of normal, healthy, intelligent people, then from them, a group of near geniuses, and finally a real genius who will fly his ship to Mars Center, and redeem Earth.

"It was the selfishness of the planets that brought it about in its present acute form—but it was inevitable. All the near-geniuses would have gone. We accelerated the process, true, but it would have been just those intelligent, restless ones, who sought greater opportunities, who would have made the trip anyway.

"America led the Earth when she was young for just one reason. She was populated by only those people who had intelligence enough to earn their passage-money, who had ambition enough to seek new opportunity, and brains enough to permit them to cut loose from the land where they were born. America lost her advantage slowly as a new race of settled people rose. For a time, all the restless, driving genes of the Caucasian race were concentrated in America. In Europe, there remained the stupid, land-loving peasant who could not see beyond the horizon.

"The planets inevitably were populated by a race of men who could see beyond the horizon, even beyond the skies, and up to the stars. They inevitably got the restless, ambitious men and women who sought new room for their abilities.

"Why—Earth was doomed to decay when Laurie sent his first rocket to Mars nearly seven hundred years ago. We of the planets made it worse still by our selection, generation after generation, of the finest and best blood Earth had to offer.

"Now, we are leaving Earth. We will send no ships. We will send no messages, nor receive any from Earth. We will send no men. Most of all, we will take none. Thirty generations brought about the downfall of Earth. Thirty more may see it rebuilt.

"We leave within a month. I leave this evening.

"We hope to hear from you, or better, from the people of Earth, in another seven or eight hundred years. But no matter how long it may take, Earth will be completely isolated so far as we are concerned. It is impossible for us to do any positive thing to aid Earth. Only time, and generations of men can do it.

"One other thing," he added with a faint smile. "I may hope to greet the first man of the New Earth. James Steven Munro has discovered a system of prolonging life for a period as yet unknown. I am proud to say that I am one of the few who have been chosen to receive this treatment.

"We of the planets have decided, thanks to the example of Earth, that death is a necessary evil. It alone purges the race, and makes room for the new generations. Only the coming of new, and newer generations can bring the new and better men. Evolution did not stop when men arose from the mud.

"We have seen evolution. You have seen the short, inhumanly powerful men of Jupiter, and the lean, dry, dark men of Mars.

"But I may live to greet the first of the new men of Earth.

"Now I am leaving. The decision is final."

"Do you mean to say that Interplanetary considers Earth unworthy of their high and mighty society?" roared Wallowy, his face crimson with rage.

Montgommery stood up slowly, and smiled at him.

"I'm afraid it does. Of yours, at any rate, I might add, for your interested consideration that we thought of teaching you how to live for centuries. It would prevent any increase in your intelligence. If you become intelligent, you may prevent the re-evolution of intelligence in the Plehbs. We decided against it, because you would probably give it to the Plehbs also, so that new workers would not have to be trained, so that less time would be lost during their infancy. That would prevent new generations, so we decided against it."

Montgommery smiled, and despite the storm of anger bellowing from enraged and life hungry men, he walked out, protected by the same, short, powerful Jovian guard he had previously mentioned.

The interplanetary transport-cruiser "Terra" rose gently, its weight destroyed, and lifted across the white, calm tip of Mt. Blanc. Her ion rockets flared to pale bluish flames as she shot upward.

Interplanetary was leaving Earth.

END OF PROLOGUE

CHAPTER ONE

BRAVELY the nine-year-old boy swung along the passages, through the almost deserted main corridors, past the roaring workshops. Polshin guards stationed here and there paid little attention to him. Plehb workers plodding about their work heavily, or walking more briskly, carrying messages, paid no attention to him. He was the sole care of his parents and himself. No one would pay any attention if one more child was caught in a machine or crushed under a heavy truck

Bruce Lawry, actually was considerably frightened, for he had bravely determined to reach the far-away Deserted Passages.

Jon Lawry, Bruce's father had told him about those Deserted Passages. Jon was a mechanician, a Plehb of the 'A class' in consequence, and fairly free to roam, his blue garb a protection from Polshin guards. Jon had seen and entered these deserted passages, when a mysterious short circuit in a power circuit had to be located. Far back in the Deserted Passages, the power line had long since been dead-ended, and never removed. A fall of stone from the passage roof had shorted it. Bruce was determined to see them. He had told Don he would. He had taken one of his father's little light-tubes so that he could see.

It was nearly four miles across the city, and all the distance had to be traversed on foot. Once, his father had told him, the streets had moved, and you could ride on them, but that had been stopped, to discourage the wandering of the Plehbs.

His father, had been apprenticed to a man who knew the story of the great city of N'yak of long ago. Then, his father had told him not only the Polshins had surface homes, but even the Plehbs had lived above ground. Only because it was cheaper to create artificial light from atomic power and maintain air conditioning, than to maintain both of these and also buildings that the weather constantly wore down, had the Plehbs been moved below the surface, into the rocks.

Jon had even been to the surface sometimes, to fix power lines leading to the Polshin homes.

Bruce walked more slowly as he came at last to the edge of the city. There were few people in the streets here now. The Polshin guards were far apart, and the light-tubes were scanty. Bruce looked down the corridor he was following and saw where the light ended. There was no Polshin stationed there, for it was a little side street where no people lived.

HURRIEDLY Bruce scuttled beyond the lighted zone, and looked back. No Polshin had seen him. He went on, stumbling in the dark, afraid to light his hand-torch. Something tripped him suddenly, and he fell with a little cry of fear. Quickly he turned his light on it. It was a strange, white, latticework of rounded bars. It was only when he saw that it was an outline, about his own size, and that, draped over it was the metal-cord belt such as he wore, that he realized what it must be—a skeleton.

He almost went back. But he looked and saw there was no light-tube beside this skeleton, and determinedly he started on. He wondered how many more might have come this way, and died.

With the super-developed sense of direction he had acquired from many walks about the lighted part of the city, he felt no fear of getting lost. Instead he went on and on, his light-tube glowing now.

He passed long rows of deserted dwellings. Then he came to a section, the like of which he had never seen. The corridor had grown wider and wider as he advanced, with incoming passages adding to it. Here at last he came to a great Cube, far greater than Cube Center in the part of the city he knew. In the center of the Cube was a building, not made of the universal granite, gray and cold, but of white stone, of marble had he known it. It was utterly different from anything he had ever seen, beautiful and clean and white. In the spread light of the tiny, but wonderfully powerful hand-light, he could dimly see the graceful columns and the roof. That was something he had never seen before, in this weather-less place. He did not know that this was a copy of Greek architecture.

Breathlessly, excited as he had never been before, he looked around him. The whole Cube was lined with various great glass windows, far larger than he had ever seen before. They were dark now, and lonely little heaps of rubbish lay behind them, he could not guess their purpose.

Cautiously he made his way toward the beautiful white building. There was rubbish on the stone floor of the great Cube. Over it he picked his way with the aid of the little light-tube and went up the broad, foot-worn steps of the library. This library was very old, even he knew that. He knew more than most children of that thirty-fourth century civilization would have known. He could read the inscription above the door, even though it meant little to him, "INTERPLANETARY LIBRARY FOUNDATION." Foundation he understood. His father had taught him to read, for Jon Lawry, being a mechanician, had to be able to read meters, and other things, as had his predecessors, and so the art of reading had been handed down among the mechanicians. Bruce knew foundation only as a heavy base one put machines on. He looked around for the machine, and wondered what kind of thing it could have been that had been set on this beautiful structure.

INTERPLANETARY meant nothing to him. He did not know what a planet was. Library meant as little, for the Plehbs had forgotten libraries and printed literature almost entirely, and the little they knew was the simple technical material they needed. Actually Bruce's mother, Marta, had taught him reading more than his father had, though his father had begun his instruction, for Marta was a worker in the chemical plants. She had nearly half a dozen books, books on thin metal plates, worn and broken now, for they were some four hundred and fifty years old. These were the only books Bruce knew. Libraries were unheard of among the Plehbs.

Bruce stared at the great bronze doors. Cautiously he pulled at one. It did not open. The grill of the gate was far too fine-meshed for him to slip through, and there were no windows in the building. Inside he could see the smooth layer of gray dust on the white stone, and long racks, a series of great tables, and here and there a low desk. It was very dark, save where his light touched it. He wanted very much to get in.

Suddenly he turned his attention to the lock. It was steel, bright, rustless steel, far too well made to be opened by his efforts. Perhaps somewhere there still existed a key for that lock, but no man on all Earth could have said where it might be. But Bruce was a mechanician, his mind was sharp, and trained to mechanical and electrical thoughts. Confidently he examined the door then he turned, and made his way back through the trash and litter of the Cube. Hunting, he finally found what he wanted, a bent piece of metal some six inches long. Fearfully he made his way to the door, stripped off his single garment, and wrapped his hand and the light-tube in it. Then with the other hand he removed the tiny glowing gas-tube from the device, and carefully inserted the bent metal, carefully protected with some mouldering cloth. In a moment he had located the thinnest of the metal bars of the grill.

A sudden groaning hum came from his light-tube as he made the contact, a popping and crackle of sparks, and a shower of incandescent metal fell on his cloth wrapped hand. Some burned his bare body—but the grill bar parted. Again he applied his light-tube, another bar gave way. Three more bars he fused. Then he stopped, and replaced the gas-tube. It didn't fit well now, for even the resistant light-tube was somewhat burned, and it didn't glow very brightly any longer, for the charge was nearly used. He knew though that it would burn satisfactorily for another four hours, and then he would have the emergency cell left for half an hour more.

TUGGING, straining with all his power, he pulled the broken bars aside. He crept inside and looked about him. Now he could see the stacks, and with a soft intake of breath he realized they were books. Books in such quantities as he had never imagined! Rapidly he went to them, and read their titles.

"T-h-e D-e-v-e-l-o-p-m-e-n-t o-f I-n-t-e-r-p-l-a-n-e-t-a-r-y C-o-l-o-n-i-z-a-t-i-o-n," he spelled out. But he didn't know what it was. So he took down the book and looked at it. Then he put it back, realizing he did not know anything about it at all and looked at other shelves.

Three hours later his light was growing very dim, and he realized he must hurry back to the lighted ways soon. Regretfully he turned away, and started homeward. But he determined that this Library, the meaning of which he knew now, was to be his secret, shared only with Don Wade. They would come back here, and bring fresh light-tubes with them, and they would learn what was in all those thousands of books.

Why, they might learn even what made the Burners give off their silent, hot flame endlessly, and the great surging currents. Nobody knew that anymore, but Jon Lawry had said, "They have forgotten. Once men knew, but they have all forgotten now. And the books are lost. They must have told once upon a time. Once, men were wiser than now."

CHAPTER TWO

DOT STEEL was the third person to enter the library after the seven centuries of desertion. Bruce brought Don back with him that next day. Children had their work to do too soon enough in life. By the time he was twelve, Bruce was apprenticed to his father in the mechanics business. Time and again he amazed his father with work Jon could not do. By then he had read some of the books in that library, and what had been a child's secret from the first day, became even more of a secret. And from them he had learned the secrets of the machines Jon repaired blindly by rule. They were to him, just as to Don Wade, an escape. In the books they left the grinding labor of the year 3340 and went back through time to the days when Earth was great.

An even deeper secret it was as they advanced to adolescence. Then, as their apprenticeship approached an end, their maturing minds began to realize more and more fully the significance of this thing. They realized the true inheritance of mankind. Bruce had studied the technical books, both because they lay along the field of his work and because in them lay his interests. He knew how the Burners worked, splitting the atom, and releasing the protons and electrons in, flying streams, to give off the tremendous currents that were the lifeblood of their civilization.

Wade had studied the historical books, he had gathered more and more a true picture of what the human race had been. But one problem was left in his mind. What had happened? Why had men fallen so, and fallen so completely and abruptly? In 2695, dozens of books were placed on the shelves. In 2697, the last book had been placed there. The library records ended in 2703. What had brought about this tremendous and abrupt fall, from a vast civilization that spread to every planet of the system, to a tiny shrunken thing that could not maintain itself at its high level for even one brief decade? Had men been afflicted with some titanic system-wide plague? Why was there absolutely no record of this tremendous, world-shaking change?

Don, more than Bruce, was absorbed in this problem. Don was the student, the sociologist. Bruce was the scientist. To Bruce came the sheer, thrilling exultation of intellectual brilliance as he read of the scientific achievements of the Old Days. When men had come face to face with an absolutely impassable boundary—why they had simply dodged under it or over it or crept around it. Nothing had stopped man then, it seemed. In the greatness of Earth, Man had sought, and found the secret of the energy of exploding atoms. One of the things that had given Bruce the keenest joy was the infinite subtlety with which men had attacked the problem of X-rays. No substance could be ruled with lines so close together as to produce a diffraction grating such as was used in light study. So—man had used the natural, regularly spaced crystal-molecules in substances as his diffraction grating X-rays could not be reflected by a mirror, or concentrated by a lens to form an image. Yet man had used crystals to focus X-rays to make pictures of things too minute to be caught by light.

Bruce did not wonder at it, it seemed perfectly natural to him, but he was able to understand and follow with ease the deepest thoughts of those greatest thinkers of the Old Days.

Why shouldn't he, he would have thought? They were men, he was a man—so why not?

THE Planets had done better by Earth, in leaving her, than they had guessed. Wheat, strong and healthy, planted in fertile ground, produces lavishly. But *all* the wheat grows, weak with the good, and gradually the yield falls to that of ordinary wheat in ordinary ground. Weak, poor wheat, in poor, lean ground, will grow very poorly. The crop will be nearly nothing. But with a few generations, it rises to a more normal level. Now if that wheat be transplanted to good land, the yield will be enormous, because that harsh, poor land has killed out the weaklings, the unresistant, and only strong, vigorous stock could survive.

The planets had concentrated all the weakness of the race on Earth. All the weakness of the race had killed itself by its very weakness. Now, in the thirty-fourth century, a tiny population of scarcely two hundred million remained of Earth's former three billion. But those two hundred million were far above the average of the twentieth century, before the great dividing began.

Bruce and Don had studied, each finding a vast interest and release in these books. More and more they realized they must keep it secret, lest the Polshins find it, and destroy them as possible revolutionists. No other humans knew of these finds.

And that was why Dot Steel was finally brought. Don met her when doing some special work for the Metals Department. They had worked together, talked together— and soon they loved together. Don, just twenty-two, was tall and wirely powerful, his keen, pleasant face framed in golden blond hair. He wore the Blue of a Class A Plehb, and, for that matter, so did Dot Steel. There was no law that forced them to marry within their own Plehb-class, but the Class A

Plehbs, being in similar lines of work, tended to come more together, they lived in the same parts of the city, and there was a natural tendency to intermarry.

Dot Steel was twenty when they met, five feet two in height, slim, as soft and graceful as a cat. Her hair was black as the Deserted Corridors and shiny as lacquer. Her lips were full and red, and her black eyes seemed to challenge Don to love her.

He did, he loved her whole-heartedly. He'd have gone to the Mating Office with her within a week of the day he met her, but that was still only a first-grade apprentice. In six months he was to get his Class C Masters' papers, and with them in hand he could petition the local Polshin for a separate apartment, and on mating he would be granted, with his wife, a two-week holiday. So they had not gone at once to the Mating Office.

Dot Steel wanted to. She cared only for the moment, and she wanted Don, wanted him as only a Plehb, who had little in life to long for, could want anything. She wanted to be with him, and feel him near her. Not some time, but now.

AND Don, with the keener, more powerful mind, realized it would be far better if they started their own home, instead of bringing a wife to live with his own parents. Further, now, as a Class One apprentice, he and his wife were entitled to but one week of vacation.

Dot began to doubt him, she grew suspicious of his love. And further, she knew when his hours of rest came, she knew he had twelve full hours off every day, yet never did he spend more than three with her, and then only once a week. The other days, he limited himself to one hour—and vanished. Try as she would, coax as she would, she could not learn where he spent the other time.

So one day when Don Wade called, expecting three hours with his own girl—she was cold and angry, she accused him of spending nearly all his time with another girl.

"I know, I know. You say you don't—but where *do* you go? Have you ever told me? Have you ever denied even that you were free those hours? One hour—then you are gone. You do not love—and you do not even play fair with the other girl, the one you must love better, for you spend most of your time with her."

"Oh, Dot, darling. I don't, I love you, and only you, I—"

"Then why don't you stay with me? Why do you always leave? You go off with Bruce—and stay away. You have lovers together."

"Sweetheart, in this town you know that couldn't be true," Don smiled. "You'd have heard the 'truth' from the neighbors."

"I have," snapped the girl. "They all know you leave me. That's why it's so unbearable. If you love me and not some other girl, prove it. Take me where you have been going."

That was final. Either Dot went where Don spent all his time—or Don could spend *all* his time there so far as she was concerned.

In despair, Don turned to the telephone system. Bruce, now a Master Mechanician, was necessarily available by phone.

"We must show her, Bruce. It is your discovery—shall we take her?"

"Of course, Don, if it means your happiness you need not have asked me. Shall I come along?"

"Will you? I'm afraid," he laughed ruefully, "she would not believe my word in her present mood."

THEY started in an hour, Bruce leading the way in his blue Masters' garb with its gold star. Down half-lighted back passages, then through a series of apartments long deserted that stood right on the border line between the deserted and the populated regions, missing the Polshin guards as always. Then down the familiar passages to the Great Cube. It was Laurie Cube as Bruce knew now. As they came to it, the great gas-tubes lighted suddenly. A little scream of surprise came from Dot. Those miles of black, mysterious corridors, deserted for centuries, had been all she could stand. Only her determination to see where Don was leading her drove her on. As they came on, she became convinced that Don was taking her here that he might scare her, make her afraid to go through with it. Then always he could say when he left her that he was going to the place he would have taken her had she not been afraid.

As the lights blazed up suddenly, mysteriously, at their approach, her nerves almost gave way altogether.

"It's all right honey—just an automatic photo-cell device. Bruce arranged to light it at our approach."

"Oh," she gasped, then "oh—how beautiful!"

In the full light of the light-tubes, the little Greek temple of white silica stone shone like a great jewel, in a dark setting. About it the dark granite absorbed the light, it alone reflected it and seemed to glow of its own light.

Warm yellowish light shone from the doorway of the library now. Inside was the clean white light of the reading lights, but here the warmth of the yellowish light seemed to welcome them.

Rapidly they advanced, and Dot Steel entered the library, the third human to enter it since this region had been deserted six centuries before.

"In-ter-plan-et-ary Li-brar-y Foun-dati-on. What's that mean? What is this place?"

"A library is a place where books are kept, darling. Bruce found this place when he was a small boy, and ever since we have been coming here, studying, reading the books of the Old Days. Darling, we know more about this city here than the Polshins. We know more about the machines than any other man living. These books have kept all the knowledge that men had forgotten. We have learned it again."

"Books?" the girl cried. "Just books?" She looked into the library now, looked about at the shelves of books, racked in thousands and thousands. The tables were strewn here and there with sheets of paper, pencils, calculating machines.

"JUST books," smiled Bruce, his deep voice smiling with him. "But you shouldn't say 'just' books. Books are something you have not learned to understand. Man practically lost books for seven centuries. Why, I don't know. And because he lost Books, he lost everything. He lost freedom, and wisdom and judgment. He lost ease and happiness.

"The books can teach him to win them back."

"I tried to read a book once," said Dot, her suspicions returning. "It was very uninteresting. It was so uninteresting I went to sleep, and was nearly late to work. I don't believe you come here. No one could be so interested in books as you pretend."

"But we are, Dot. That is how we have gotten our advancement so quickly. Don't you remember Bruce got his Master's Papers because he fixed a broken burner that no other Mechanician could fix. He could fix it because he knew how those machines worked. He alone of all men knows why they do what they do. I have gotten my papers rapidly, because I have taken from these books knowledge that has been lost for centuries, and put it to use."

"But that doesn't make me believe you are so interested you come here day after day and read—read books," she said the last words with scorn.

"Sweetheart, you have never read books. You don't know the romance and the mystery that surrounds them, and the things they say. What were the Old Days like—and why did they end? Who are the Polshins? Who are the Plehbs? Do you know that 'Polshin' comes from a corruption of the old word 'Politician,' a man who sought to gain some public office? Oh—but you don't know what a public office is.

"There are mysteries and wonders in those books."

"I read one," insisted Dot. "It was very uninteresting."

"Dot," said Bruce, "there are one hundred and fourteen thousand books in this library. There are one hundred and three thousand different books—no two alike. You read one. You know how you hate Jak Studds. Would you say because Jak Studds was hateful, that all Plehbs are hateful? Be fair. Because one book is uninteresting to one very small, and very pretty little girl, that does not mean that one hundred and three thousand books are all very uninteresting to a man."

"Well—maybe. But then why is Don so unwilling to go to the Mating Office with me?" she launched her attack suddenly along different lines.

"Dot, Dot—you know I'm not unwilling to go there with you," Don cried, wrapping her suddenly in his arms, and turning her face up to his. "There's nothing I want more— except perhaps your happiness. And that, I think, I can best assure by waiting a little longer."

"NOOO—you can't—you can't," she suddenly sobbed, and hugged him harder, burying her face suddenly on his chest. "I—I want you Don—I want you *now!*"

Don lifted her face again. "If you want me so much, now, as much as I want you maybe, why—I guess we can get to the Mating Office in half an hour."

But Dot didn't stop crying. She cried harder, and hugged him harder, and began to dance. "Let's go—Let's go—"

CHAPTER THREE

THERE were three couples ahead of them when they reached the Mating Office. All of them were trying to look bored and indifferent. All of them were being very stiff and wooden. The couple in the Blue were being Recorded first. A mixed couple, a man in Blue and a girl of the Greens was next, then a Green pair, and finally a pair of big, powerful-bodied Grays.

Each couple was accompanied by a Master of his class to act as witness and identifier. The Blues' witness was evidently the girl's father, and he was quite as flustered as the pair themselves. The Plehb clerk behind the bench looked at him with a bit of annoyance, but not too much, for he was a second class blue, while the Master was, of course, a first-class. Finally the pair moved away, to the accompaniment of chuckles and snickers of half-suppressed laughter from the Polshin Guards standing at the door.

One of the Polshins left his post long enough to press his seal-ring on the wax, and returned, his soft scarlet cloak flapping about his legs.

This guard-duty was the one task the Polshin men performed in all their lives. For two years they were forced to do the strenuous job of standing or sitting about in the Plehb sections and guarding the Polshin's interests. Usually they went in pairs, for company. Each was armed with a shock-rod, but it meant nothing, for they were seldom needed. Their duty in this office was merely to put a Polshin stamp of approval on the Mating Record—and collect their fees. Two, lest the duty be too boring.

The mixed couple, accompanied by a Blue Master, was up now. The Master in this case was evidently the young man's Apprentice-master. The records were entered speedily, and the three departed. The green couple followed, as another couple came behind Dot and Don. Then—Omallin came in. Omallin's entrance at that precise moment was as mighty a force in the course of human history, as Montgommery's speech on the "Independence of Mars," or that later speech of the later Montgommery on the "Isolation of Earth." Omallin was the local Polshin leader, N'Yak's Polshin Chief. He was round, and short and fat, his face was red and fat, his hair faded, and missing on top altogether, so his pink, shiny skull showed. His fifty-three years of utter unrestraint showed in the bleary, pig-eyes, in the flabby, fat face and the flabby, fat belly. He waddled when he walked, and his voice was high-pitched and unpleasant. But he was followed by a retinue of lesser Polshins, bowing morally, intellectually, and physically to this scarlet-cloaked, monstrosity. His once sharp hawk's nose was half buried in the soft fat of his face, and the sharp chin, whose evolution marked the evolution of man, was lost in rolling, quivering fat.

Omallin entered, and the Polshin guards sprang to the straightest of attention. The Plehb clerk bowed low, and the other Plehbs in the room inclined their heads.

Omallin nodded grandly. The Polshin Guards relaxed, the Plehbs straightened again. "Plehb, how many matings this month?" demanded the Polshin Leader.

"Six thousand four hundred and thirty-nine, Polshin Sir," replied the clerk.

"The rate is rising?"

"Yes, Polshin Sir."

"HMM—maybe, Karrody, I will admit your request to open some of the Deserted Passages to Council. Hmm—" Omallin looked around him.

Dot Steel had, with the other Plehbs, sunk back to the less lighted portion of the room, but the softer light merely enhanced and softened her beauty. Omallin's wandering eyes suddenly focused. A slow smile came across the fat face.

"By Gah—a beauty. Plehb, come here."

Dot Steel's richly colored face went white as the clerk's papers. Her body was suddenly trembling, her eyes opened, dilated slowly. But she did not move.

The Polshin Guard nearest the girl stepped over abruptly. "Plehb, move when you're ordered," he snapped. A touch of the shock-rod and the girl jumped violently. With a little whimper she turned and started for the door on flying feet. The Polshin guard caught her, just as Bruce Lawry, his cold gray eyes blazing caught Don Wade. "Fool," he whispered, "you cannot help by fighting. It will only be death."

The Polshin guard brought Dot Steel toward Omallin. Omallin's fat hand reached up, caught the fastener of the girl's suit, a swift crinkle of sound and the single garment fell away, leaving her white body under the lights.

Omallin's eyes seemed to lose their bleariness for a moment.

"Ahh—" he said softly. "Send her to Infirmary Five for the treatment then to my place—she is very nice."

The girl collapsed slowly, gently to the floor, and lay quiet as Omallin walked out of the room. The Plehbs in the room were tensely quiet as the grinning Polshin Guards picked up the girl. Passing his hands over her, one turned to his companion with a broader grin. "Old Omallin—"

White faced, frozen Don exploded into life so suddenly that Bruce did not even feel the warning tensing of his muscles. One blow of his fist, backed by the work-hardened muscles of a strong man, sent the Polshin Guard flying half across the room.

One touch of the other's shock-rod jerked Wade into abrupt unconsciousness. His lax body fell across Dot Steel. Raging, holding his near-broken jaw, the first Polshin started across the room, his shock-rod glowing now with the blue fire that meant death at its touch.

"Wait, Mark. The poor fool was crazy. He's a Blue, and worth something. Losing his woman made him kind of crazy, don't kill him."

"Out of the way—that Plehb-spawned maggot *struck* me! No Plehb can—"

"Let him live, Mark, let him live. He was crazy. Don't worry. He's paying for it."

* * *

IT was hours later when Don Wade woke. Bruce was leaning over him, his eyes cold and clear. There was a hypodermic needle in his hand.

"Dot," groaned Wade. Abruptly he sat up. He stared about him. He was in the Library now, lying on one of the tables.

"Lie back, Don. You almost died anyway. Believe it or not, the interference of a Polshin saved your life."

"Where's Dot?"

"She's gone, Don," replied Bruce steadily. "You know that."

Don's eyes began to smolder with a colder, saner hate now. "I'm going to get her back. These maps—the old maps! They will show where Infirmary is, and I'll bring her back!"

"No, Don. You won't. Listen to me, Don. You aren't prepared to bring her back. You couldn't get to her in the first place. In the second, you would not be able to bring her away now. She's been operated on by now. She will be unable to move for days. If you did reach her, and escape with her, where could you go? I have thought of all this.

While I was getting that stuff to revive you from the old Interplanetary Hospital, I thought that out.

"Don, you will have to lose Dot. I know more of medicine now than do those doctors of Infirmary Five. They are trained only by what is remembered from the Old Days. I know all that is known of the Old Days—more than they do. Listen, I will tell you what will happen. Dot is not like most of the Plehb girls taken. She is not the first but she will be almost the last. Dot will become conscious when the anesthetic wears off about two days from now. Then she will know what has happened. She will be treated. And she will die because she does not want to live. Nothing they knew even in the Old Days would have been able to make her whole again, so even if you could reach her, it would avail you nothing, because Dot would not want to live, and she would die. When a human not only does not fight for life, but seeks death, that human will die, even though they be in sound health. With a wound, death is inevitable. Dot is lost, Don."

For a long minute Don sat in silent, blank-faced thought. Slowly he sank back. "Yes. She is, I guess. I have read that too. And I know Dot." He smiled faintly at Bruce. "What will work for her, will work for me, Bruce. I do not want to live."

Bruce's eyes just hardened. "I thought of that, too. I would not have saved you if I had not known you would want very much to live. Don, you want to live because you know more than any other living human. You know the secrets of the old days, and we can learn more. With them— *We will not only destroy Omallin, but we will destroy the whole Polshin order:* we will bring back the Old Days!"

SLOWLY Don's eyes lit up again, and again he sat up. "Use these secrets of the Old Days—to end Omallin and the Polshins. Yes, Bruce. I want very much to live."

His voice was so coldly, precisely deadly, Bruce looked at him sharply. Don spoke again. "It will take years, won't it, Bruce? We cannot do it alone, for then it would not stay done. The other Plehb girls would be seen by other Omallins, and not want to go on living. No, it will take years, and we must be very careful. We must make all the Plehbs in N'Yak help us first. Then—I wonder if the old cities still exist, like this one. Shkaga and Washton, San Franco and London. Somehow, Bruce, we must learn, and start in all those cities, so that *all* the Polshins everywhere are destroyed.

"And first we must learn *all* the secrets of the Old Days, and more too, if possible. I think perhaps we can. We will open the old Interplanetary Laboratories. Somehow we must build an atomic cruiser, for I know that while we have seen only the pleasure cruisers of the Polshins, they must have, somewhere, the old atomic cruisers. We will need powerful weapons if we are to regain the surface for the Plehbs."

"I thought you would agree with me, Don. Yes, it will take years. And all those years you must keep out of the sight of the Polshin Guards, for one of those two in the Office there will look for you. The one you hit. The other saved your life."

"For that, perhaps I should thank him. If he did not, I would not have had this opportunity." Don's cold, precise voice seemed with him permanently now.

CHAPTER FOUR

DON WADE began the study of mass psychology, and the psychology of the individual that day, while Bruce began the study of the maps with more care. The power they were using to light the library and the Laurie Cube outside, they had simply stolen from the old power-lines that had never been torn out. But now, Bruce realized, he would want vastly more power, power to light and operate the buildings. For they had decided that some small part of this deserted section was going to be restored to the beauty it must have had before the Great Catastrophe, as they had come to call that period of sudden fall from Earth's greatness, the sudden change from the Old Days.

Bob Steel, Dot's brother, was their first recruit, and Jon Lawry their second. Bob Steel was a Master of Direction, and a class A Blue. And he hated the Polshins with as deadly a hate as did Don Wade. With Wade he began to read the old books, and to learn what had been before. He quickly appreciated the mystery and romance of them. And—their possibilities for revenge, and for reinstatement of the Old Days. Old Jon read the books, and with ecstatic joy learned again the secrets forgotten by men for more than six Centuries. He reveled in knowing. With difficulty he restrained himself from showing his knowledge at every job he was called on, and from calling on Bruce's far greater knowledge. Bruce had trained himself through years to study to a point that equaled the learning of any physicist of the Old Days. To him the atomic engines were clear, and straightforward in their action.

The Polshins had had, years and centuries ago, a spy system. That had been discarded long ago. When first the semi-Plehbs, the small property owners and near-genius trade intellects had been suppressed almost immediately after Interplanetary's complete withdrawal, there had been violent, crafty rebellion, led by these intelligent ones. Soon, though, they had been killed off, had died out, or by intermarriage with the weaklings, both in mind and spirit, the last revolutionary tendencies had been stamped out. The far-reaching spy system of those days had died out with it. Gradually the televiso-system fell into decay, and failed utterly. The telephone system was simpler, needed less intelligence for its operation, and was maintained because the Polshins needed rapid communication at times of emergencies. The Masters were connected by telephone system, but that had, at first been watched with the greatest care, lest it be used for plotting. Finally even this had stopped.

Now, in 3350, there was no check on the Plehbs, because there seemed to be no need for it. The Plehbs had no unification whatever, no common leaders save the Polshins.

But, unnoted by the Polshins, intelligence had risen again. The dampness of stupidity had dried out of the powder and Bruce was the fulminate cap that would set it off. Omallin had pounded the cap. Already the trains of fire were streaking out through the loose mass of highly intelligent and explosive men. All they needed was to be shown what *could* be—and they would demand it.

In a month, Bruce and Jon, and a dozen other master mechanicians had restored the great power station in the Mahtan section of the city, the long deserted part, that part furthest from the inhabited portion. There were lights there now, the great atomic burners supplying plentiful power. And—the elevators had been restored to operation, the moving walks moved again. There were goods in the show-windows, goods manufactured in the hidden plants in that deserted section by the skilled Plehbs who had been converted to the movement.

THE Mahtan section lived and breathed with a surface semblance of the old life. The televiso-system was in full operation here, and century-old reels of televise-plays, stored in the magnetism of thin steel ribbons, were again in action, the theatres were lighted and showing scenes of the Old Days.

These educated the people to the old life far more quickly than the finest of orators could have educated them. Educational reels showed the whole Solar System, how it was made up, and how it worked. Newsreels showed the mighty jungles of Venus, the blazing, smoking rocks of Mercury, the yellow-red deserts of Mars, and their gleaming cities. They saw the ultra-powerful, squat men of Jupiter, and the lean, tall, tanned men of Mars. The mighty glaciers of Athena's frozen airs, and her broad rivers of liquid helium flowed again across Terrestrial screens.

They rode again in the early rockets, then in the mightiest of the great space liners of seven centuries before.

And Don Wade spoke. Don had trained himself with the aid of the old books, and with the patient, deadly precision of a man who's life is directed to one end, the destruction of a hated system. Normally when he spoke now, his voice held only that cold deadliness. But when he spoke to his audiences, it was rich, and strong. It told the men what they could be. Blues and Greens were admitted, but as yet no Grays, for Don Wade had one important message to give, and no Gray would have been intelligent enough to obey.

"Do not let any Polshin, for whatever reason, even gain suspicion that in the slightest degree, your ideas have been changed."

There was everything to win. Those Plehbs, seeing the city alive, the walks moving freely once more, the televiso news working, admitted freely now to the half-dozen libraries that had been found, did change. But they were chosen Plehbs, too. Not over a thousand at any time were allowed to enter the Deserted Passages. There must be no sudden decrease in the population of the inhabited section.

And other, side-separated routes were found for entering the deserted section. There were a score or more Plehbs who had permanently left the old section, and lived now as guards and watchmen at the entrances to the new. Televiso-systems kept them connected with Bruce's headquarters.

Bruce had established himself. He was one of those who no longer lived in the old section, but on one of the lowest levels of the Mahtan section. Deep down here, two levels below the power plant, was the Interplanetary Research Laboratory. When Interplanetary had maintained its offices on Earth, these laboratories had been the finest research organizations on the planet. They had been used for research in physics, in chemistry and biology, and for human research, for testing applicants for emigration. When Interplanetary had left that laboratory had been simply closed down. The Polshins had not been interested in research—and they could have found no adequate scientists to populate it, had they been so inclined.

BRUCE found it. And Bruce repopulated it. From the Master Kem class, he drew chemists, from the Master Meks, he drew mechanicians and electricians. From the Master Bios, he drew his biologists. Then he set them all, nearly fifty of the most intelligent Plehbs, the most intelligent Terrestrians, working on the books and records he found here; the more advanced books in Physics he read himself, the last records, the reports and scientific publications that had been printed on Mars and Jupiter.

"For there is one problem that will, when solved, give us the things we need—real power.

"We must remember this. The old revolutions were always stamped out by two methods: shutting off the airflow, and pumping in heat till the Plehbs nearly suffocated. They had to stop. All those controls are still in the hands of the Polshins at the surface. They still know how to use them, I'll bet. Then they turned off all the power, so that darkness and utter lack of energy forced submission and the deliverance of the leaders to them.

"Our first necessity is independent power. We can't possibly build new atomic burners. Remember the 'infuse' lining of the burners, and of the stop plates is a substance we cannot make here. We must have the Jovian elements. We must seek a new answer to the old problem of power. Chemical fuels simply won't do. Accumulators, marvelous as they are, aren't enough.

"Besides, we must have a greater power than the Polshins. And they have the atomic cruisers. Don, the atom contains the secret. That, was the one problem that was not fully solved in the Old Days. I think I have a chance, where they failed, because I have learned not at the time, but centuries later, and I have gotten a perspective that they did not have. I have learned across all the centuries. Toward the end of the Old Days they were treating the atom more and more as a particle, but several centuries before that, they had considered it more as a series of waves.

"The treatment of the atom as a particle, however, brought them the energy of the atom, while the treatment as a wave brought them nothing whatever.

"The treatment as a particle brought them a particle of the energy. Think of it this way: A thousand tons of water is a mile above you. You can extract the potential energy of that water as it falls, by treating it as a mass. But if you treat it as an enormous number of atoms and take out its atomic energy, you get infinitely more energy.

"The break-up of an atom in the Burners yields electrical energy as charges. The Burners simply break up the atom the way a man might take apart the plates of an accumulator, and discharge each plate separately. In the burner the atom is exploded, in a tremendous magnetic field. The protons and electrons, which composed the atom, are hurled apart and scattered like the fragments of a bursting shell. Before that energy can become available, as electricity, the particles must be separated into two types, the positive protons going one place and the negative electrons another. The magnetic field does this, it directs the protons one way, because they are moving positive charges, and the electrons the other, because they are moving negative charges. The two streams move in opposite directions around the center of the magnetic fields and strike the 'infuse' collector plates. They build up a charge on these plates that tends to repel the incoming particles. The charge reaches about a million volts, and then stays there, for at that voltage the repulsion is so great that the incoming protons or electrons are almost stopped before striking. If we draw off power, the voltage falls to just such an extent as will allow such a number of protons and electrons to strike as will maintain the charge.

"BUT—the protons and electrons can't he stopped in practice, but actually strike with about twenty thousand volts velocity. That means that the kinetic impact will heat the 'infuse' plates. That's why the 'infuse' plates are made hollow, and the mercury is circulated through them. The mercury cools them, and helps stop the protons and electrons.

"Here on Earth, of coarse, we use water-cooling, and just waste the heat-energy. It's so cheap anyway, we don't have to worry about that. But in a spaceship, that heat has to be taken care of. Heat is very hard to get rid of, and while the process is 80% efficient, twenty percent of one hundred million horsepower is twenty million. A spaceship, one of the big liners, may easily use two hundred million horsepower in pulling free of Jupiter. That means a constant heat energy of forty million horse. Therefore, on spaceships, to cool them, they carry mercury cooling, use the mercury vapor so created to run turbines, and cool and recondense the mercury vapor in water turbine boilers.

"That system of atomic-electricity—mercury turbines—water turbines will take care of the normal, constant production of heat energy. By converting it to electrical energy they can use and thus get rid of it. For the short period of two hundred million horsepower used in leaving a planet, they used heat-reservoirs, tanks of liquid hydrogen, the substance, which holds the most heat, weight for weight, then they could get rid of the heat slowly. As it was, however, even the atomic cruisers had to stop at the Jovian satellites to cool off between jumps. In space, only radiation will carry away the heat you see, and radiation at any normal temperature isn't very rapid.

"Now the atomic cruisers for battle were normally in a pretty bad way if the thing went on very long, because they'd overheat. Atomic power engines would permit of about two billion horsepower in a moderate sized battle cruiser—but if they ever tried to use that, they'd have four hundred million horsepower of heat to get rid of.

"That doesn't satisfy me at all. In the first place, you are just using the potential energy of the water falling down hill. I want to find a way to use all the energy of the atom. Destroy even the remnants, so that I don't have even a hydrogen gas exhaust as the atomic engines do. I think I can see some way toward doing it. That's the goal I am heading toward now."

"What progress?" asked Don.

"Whoa—not so fast. I haven't even set up the apparatus yet. Lora Wayne is helping with it. She's a bright girl.

"You go back to your work—and I to mine. Remember, even when we have this whole city ready, we will still have to wait till we can convert the others around us."

CHAPTER FIVE

BRUCE smiled up in triumph to Lora. "That proves it, I think, doesn't it?"

"It certainly looks to me like the answer Bruce," she replied, her eyes glowing with excitement. "Can you try it out someway practically? What will it do—can you limit its action?"

"I'm sure I can. Those old mathematicians were right, when they made their calculations, but wrong when they passed on unheeding. I think this is infinitely more important than anything else we have done. The Old Days had antigravity, and we have it again." He nodded toward a large metal ball, floating unsupported in the air, a small string holding it down, and against its tendency to be thrown because of Earth's centrifugal force. "Now we have anti-reaction, you might say."

"Those waves of force though must act against something," objected Lora. "When I made the apparatus for you, I didn't see what that was going to react against."

"They don't react against some*thing,* they react against *every*thing. They are of such incomprehensible fineness that they slip through what we call matter, and space, and react against the stuff out of which our curved space is cut. They pull on all space. They push the Earth, and the Sun, on Jupiter, Mars and the Magellenic Clouds equally.

"Practically—they mean a ship without the tell-tale streams of atomic fire pushing it along. Atomic rockets are visible. These momentum waves aren't."

"It seems strange that the wave theory of atoms should lead to a means of generating momentum directly in space."

"Any correct theory of the atom must delve far deeper than surface manifestation of force we know as matter. It must take into account the real nature of *space.* Atoms aren't things—they're symptoms of space. We detect magnetic fields by their action on steel, or on an electric particle. We detect space by the existence of atoms—but atoms are merely symptoms of space as the movement of the compass needle is a symptom. The wave theory asserts, remember, that every electron, every proton, every tiniest particle is actually a series of complex waves spread through all infinite space. Over all space, these waves cancel out, the trough of one wave-system coming on the crest of another wave-set of that same electron, except in only that tiny bit of space where we can detect its effects, where the waves are not visible, and we say the electron or proton is.

"That involves space. If it described the property of space known as 'atoms' correctly, then it should describe that property of space known as 'momentum' and 'kinetic energy' correctly. Through perfectly logical derivation on the mathematics of the wave-atom, you can derive this formula of momentum, and this kinetic energy.

"THEY seemed to me the simplest means of proving or disproving the theory. Though worked out nearly fourteen hundred years ago, way back in the twentieth century, they were never tested. If a theory is good it will predict, and its predictions come true. Here is a prediction that has come true. By these momentum waves we can drive a ship silently, invisibly and almost undetectably. We are one step toward the defeat of the Polshins."

"Are you going to make a ship now?" asked Lora eagerly.

"Not yet. We have not enough men in our movement yet. Remember, we must have workers enough to operate the deserted machines here to make the vast number of things we will need. Only one hundred of us are living here permanently, and nearly a third of that number must spend the major portion of its time in services, making food on the machines, and clothing and other necessities. Another portion must spend some time on the generators, and other apparatus. Scarcely a score of us is engaged in advance work.

"Besides—I have another thing I want to work out. It may be even more important."

"What Bruce?"

Bruce turned to his laboratory assistant with a smile. These members of the new movement were not clad in blue, or green. They wore costumes of pure white, trimmed with whatever color they fancied—save only scarlet. That was Don's idea. The Scarlet would merely have broken the law. It would not have been a choice.

Lora was dressed in the white costume, trimmed with gold as was Bruce. Her jet-black hair and dark eyes made a striking contrast to it. A contrast she hoped that some day Bruce would notice.

But Bruce turned to his laboratory assistant with a smile. "The solution to another problem the men of the Old Days never solved. Television without a sending device."

"But didn't they say in the Old Days that that was impossible?"

"They did, but they also said, before it had been done, that making a machine that would fly was impossible, and that making a ship to cross space was impossible and finally that overcoming gravity was impossible. But they didn't after it had been done.

"The trouble is that you have to pick up some form of energy coming from the scene in question before you can view it. Light won't do, because bodies in between will stop it. No wave will do that is short enough to be effective in delineating the object. Radio waves will penetrate, but they are so long that they will also penetrate the body to be viewed."

"Then haven't you yourself said it was impossible?"

"WATCH. I have been working on this while you were making up that apparatus for me. It isn't fully completed. I will need a better tie-in than I have now, between the two focusing devices."

Bruce walked over to a piece of apparatus he had set up on one of the insulated benches. There were two devices, about ten feet apart, and directly between them a third. This third was flat-topped some two feet square and six inches thick. One by one Bruce turned them on. Tubes began to glow, and the recording meters mounted as the heaters began to throw out their electrons.

"She's hot. Now watch." Slowly he began turning a control dial on one of his machines. Abruptly something snapped softly into existence on the top of the little, flat, cubical box. Carefully Bruce focused it. A loud speaker began to chatter meaninglessly. As abruptly as the cloudiness had appeared, it solidified, and the speaker began to talk intelligibly.

Three men bent over their work. They were clad in the white of the Freedom Party. The delicate apparatus they were working on was taking shape. The scene was scarcely twelve inches high, but the coloring the detail, the weave of the cloth even, was in such absolute perfection that Lora gasped. Ten-inch-tall men working on an inch-long apparatus, their tiny hands functioning with perfect precision.

"What will it be when we get through, Jon? This looks to me like the old radio-receiving set circuit? Do you suppose he's going to start a radio-broadcast station again?"

"I doubt it. The Polshins might pick it up. That would be bad. It's probably something quite different. Remember that radio-frequency currents were used for thousands of purposes, from sterilizing foods under supersonic waves, to aiding medical healing and causing artificial fevers."

"Oh, *Bruce*. It's Jon, and Mark and Ted. They're six blocks away through granite walls..."

"Not all of them, Lora, not all of them. Touch one of those images there."

Timidly Lora advanced her hand and, half-frightened, touched the image of Jon's head, her finger passed easily through it—but there was a slight resistance, just the barest feeling of pressure. "Why—they're sort of solid!"

"They are. They are real images, they are part-formed electrons and protons. This device here, perfected, will mean more than anything we have ever dreamed of. It will surpass a million-fold the televise system of the Old Days.

"Every proton and every electron exists through all space. Part of the protons and electrons that compose Jon exist in this space where we are—and where the machine is. That machine cancels out part of the electron-wave, so that the rest, no longer mutually canceling, become real in our space. Those images are one one-hundred-thousandth real. I have condensed them for greater solidity. The microphone I have just turned off, picks up the tiny voices of those images, and amplifies them so that we can actually hear them.

"So far as I know—the device has no distance limits."

"Bruce—you—mean we could pick up even the planets?"

"We can. When we've built the big apparatus, and at that it is to be our first step. Because—I can reverse the process, and make myself appear. But there I am limited. I cannot appear further than one thousand miles away with any practical apparatus, and at that distance I must make myself a ghostly image fifty feet tall."

UNDER Bruce's direction, the apparatus was begun within a week. They, who made it, did not know why he installed all the elaborate timing devices, the careful clockwork. And Bruce appeared only occasionally, because most of the time he left the work to Lora.

Week after week passed. The apparatus neared completion, the Freedom movement spread through all N'yak, till more than half the Plehbs were enrolled in it, and had seen the City of the Old Days that had been gradually built up in the old Mahtan district. Still the Polshins, fat and comfortable in their assurance of power, not imagining such a movement after centuries of peace, did not feel the growing tension.

The Plehbs swung more briskly through Center Cube now, but still the Polshin guards loitered aimlessly, laughing, grinning—and occasionally still a Plehb girl disappeared as she attracted the attention of one of those guards.

Then Bruce and Don and the leaders of the movement would have their hands full, suppressing the tendency for an untimely explosion. With a realization that this was *not* just the normal course of events, came a new feeling of rebellion. Before it had seemed as inevitable as death. Now it was not.

Silently, the Freedom scientists were working. Bruce was not alone now; he was the director of a competent and growing force of scientists. One man was studying the problem of insulation against the shock-rods of the Polshins, another that of the problem of hand weapons for the Plehbs. Others were aiding Bruce in his studies of the atom. More and more Bruce was realizing that he studied not the atom, but the properties of space. The gravity-field was one of his greatest aids, the magnetic field second, yet both of these had to be handled cautiously—for their effects reached out to infinity, and powerfully to the Surface, where some Polshin might wonder at them.

Three months were needed to construct the timing devices of the great projector. Two months more saw the two focusing machines set up. A full eight months passed all together before the apparatus was ready for its first trial. All the staff that had worked on it, and many of the elected leaders of the Freedom Party were present. Based now on the Planetary Socialistic Government, elected leaders ruled the party. These elected delegates gathered with the scientists and Bruce and Don arrived.

Briefly, to the leaders, Don Wade described the intended functions of the machine. With it, they hoped first of all to see the other cities of Earth. To see whether there, too, the same system of Polshin and Plehb existed. Then, they hoped to turn their giant eye out to Mars and Venus, to see what had happened to the civilization of the Planets.

"Does it require so huge a machine for shorter ranges, such as looking at Earth-scenes?" asked one of the delegates.

"NO," Bruce replied. "I can and will, make smaller replicas of the important parts of this machine for that purpose. But this machine is intended for viewing the planets. To make that possible, I had to mount an enormously complex clockwork device to follow the planetary motions. For instance, to view a city such as Thanton on Callisto, I have first to neutralize Earth's daily rotational movement, than to neutralize the effects to Callisto's daily rotation, her orbital rotation around Jupiter, and Jupiter's orbital motion around the Sun. All of this requires an exceedingly complex apparatus. And already now, sets similar to the primary view-apparatus are in machine-production. We had to cut dies for that, and that is what took so long. That and the development work. But the technicians are now working on a similar device, which will have an illimitable theoretical range, and a practical range that would permit glimpses of life on Athena. However, this device will be but two feet square, and three inches thick.

For viewing scenes on Earth, it will be fully capable of anything we need.

"The big apparatus is ready. That stage there is ten by ten, and I will put on it life-size human images, with one ten thousandth real solidity. The subjects which are viewed will feel a slight electrical tensity, but absolutely nothing that will disturb them in the least.

"I have adjusted the controls to view the old city of Shkaga. This should be the Center Loop Cube, at the ground level."

Bruce walked to the main controls, and started them. This was, actually and really, the first time the machine as a whole had been tested. The tubes warmed, a low humming echoed momentarily from the speakers. Then—abruptly, solidification was complete. On the stage there was a portion of a building, fading off into misty unreality at the edges of the focus. Dark rubbish lay at its base, and on the pavement. There were no people on the stage; all was dark, apparently.

Bruce rapidly condensed the image. The building shrank, and the whole of the great Cube was visible, dark, and rubbish-heaped. "There are no men in this section. It is dark here, evidently. The image is lighted by our lights here. In reality, it is utterly dark. I will shift the focus." The setting blurred, seemed to shimmer and change, flashes of solid rock obscuring everything, then suddenly for an instant a flashing human figure appeared and was gone. Instantly Bruce changed the setting back.

It was a passage, lighted evidently. Half a dozen human figures in gray garb slunk disconsolately down the rocky corridor; at its end was a Polshin guard, in the deep orange the Polshins of Shkaga wore. Bruce raced down the corridor with his settings, branched to a larger one, down that, and finally reached a small Cube. There were more people here, Plehbs in gray, and dark red and dark blue. The Red here was evidently highest. But the men recognized again the Plehb and the Polshin.

IN swift succession, Bruce brought in scenes from San Franco, Washton, and a dozen other cities.

Then, in London, he found again the Polshin and the Plehb in Berlin and in Paris. In Tokyo and Peiping. In every major city, only three cities he tried showed no human life, deserted and utterly dead. Barcelona, Munich and Lyons.

"Show us what the Polshins are doing above us," called a delegate.

Bruce smiled grimly. Don Steel had prepared for this request. Not for nothing had he studied mass psychology, and he had searched for many minutes on Bruce's original model of the machine before finding the scene he knew would most quickly and effectively rouse the people. Suddenly the stage was a garden, a magnificent garden of flowers and shrubs. It was night, but soft lights made a dim illumination. In the garden were scarcely a dozen figures. Two young Polshin men, an older Polshin, and three Plehb girls in a group. The older Polshin was bleeding freely from five long gashes across his fat cheek. One of the Plehb girls was bound to a pair of young, stout trees. The Polshin had a heavy whip, and was beating at her body with all his fat strength. Her whole raiment was colored by crisscross streaks of blood, she hung loose in her bounds, perking feebly to each stroke of the whip. Low moans came from the speaker, and soft cries from the two other Plehb girls, held by the two younger men, watching the scene.

Abruptly Bruce cut the dials sharply across. A rumbling roar sounded from the speaker as there were flashed on the stage masses of jagged rock, green trees and solid mountains. An angry cry mounting up from the audience drowned out the sound, as the scene was established at last in a swaying forest of pines. A ruined bridge flung its broken members across a quiet stream.

"I think that will be enough of that," Bruce decided harshly. "I did not pick up the Polshins at first, because I feared some such scene. We did not have to see in order to know. We have heard all this. I think it would be best if we used now the more complex features, and viewed Mars. That is the great problem really. Have the planets suffered a like fate? Has their civilization fallen so far as has ours? Remember, we never did have anything but a straight democratic government, with no proper controls. Mars started differently. Perhaps they have not fallen quite so low."

Carefully he was setting his apparatus now, with the aid of two other trained mathematicians, one in training now to be an astronomer.

The clockwork began to hum softly, then was silenced to a barely audible purr as it got into action.

"I think we are ready. We should be within five thousand miles of the planet. You see—we do not know the exact time. We are not absolutely certain, even that we know the exact day. The old calendar was known to have defects, and we may be wrong. However—"

The lights had been turned off in the main part of the room now, and only some very carefully designed reflectors lighted the scene. Abruptly—on the stage appeared a floating ball, some five feet in diameter. Just within the limits of the machine's observation, was another ball, a tiny ball scarcely larger than a golf ball, jagged and ruggedly shadowed in the light of the spotlight flooding it. The large ball was edged with a thin, shining belt of light, bright in the powerful spotlight.

"MARS," SAID Bruce, "and even in the 'Old Days' they had nothing to equal that. We will win out, I am sure."

The planet expanded swiftly, the tiny satellite became hazy, ghostly, and vanished at the edge of the scene. Tiny spots appeared on the very slowly turning globe, spots of black and glowing light. "Those are lights on Mars," Bruce said, his voice tense. "Lights shine as lights, even in this device." The surface came nearer, toward one of those shining clumps of light. It grew, and, as it grew, the rotation of Mars became evident. The scene was turning past them. Bruce centered it again, and engaged another piece of clockwork. The scene steadied—and expanded abruptly.

They were hanging, it seemed, some ten thousand feet above the city. It was a great city of black and gold and silver and colors. The buildings towered slim and graceful, ships flew through the air around them, and into them. Only here there was no perspective. Bruce altered the setting, and the whole city, in miniature, was on the stage. Now the ships flew across the stage, and tiny, crawling dots moved in streams below.

Abruptly there appeared a section perhaps two blocks square. Only half the buildings were visible, the upper halves soaring off into the upper air. People, thousands of gaily-dressed people it seemed, flowed along on the moving ways. They were smiling, laughing, happy. A scene such as no Plehb had ever seen. Brisk, clear sounds came through the speaker, the sounds of voices mingled faintly, the hum and rush of vast business.

"Civilization didn't fall there," gasped Don. "They have all the civilization they ever had. They must have ships, spaceships—"

Bruce twisted the settings, until the scene on the stage shrunk, and grew tiny, the buildings reappeared, diminished, the city became small and the curve of the planet showed itself again. The ships sailing about the city seemed concentrated near a great open square. Bruce re-expanded the scene, centering on this view. The square was huge, so great that the great ships even seemed small. It was fully three miles on a side, the city, actually, built around it. And as they watched, they saw something dart into being on the screen, a huge something that settled on the field, and occupied a space half a mile long. A titanic space freighter.

"A spaceship!" Bruce exclaimed. "Why do they never come here if they have them? Let's look at Callisto——Venus——"

The stage grew blank with the night of space. In seconds, the giant of the Solar System appeared—mighty Jupiter, a six-foot ball, with smaller balls moving slowly about it, planetary in size themselves. Callisto—it separated, centered on the stage, then abruptly clicked into immobility as the clockwork was thrown in. In moments Bruce had located Thantor.

Thantor was a mass of moving, happy people. Small transplanetary ships moved about. Slightly larger inter-moon ships and gigantic interplanetary ships circled and moved freely.

VENUS—more ships, moving freely. Space seemed full of them. Only on the Moon and Earth were there no great spaceships.

"Why?" asked every man of himself. "Why is Earth alone deserted thus? Why was Earth left to a savage, feudal system in an ultra-machine age?"

Muttering, stupefied men left the hall. Back to their jobs, and to the men who had sent them. Back to tell of other Earth-cities under the crushing rule of the Polshins. Back to tell of Plehb girls bound and beaten to death by heavy whips in gardens of beautiful flowers and tinkling fountains. Of hundreds of millions of happy people on the other planets.

Happy people from Mercury to far out Athena. And misery, and terror and hate only on Earth. No brutal Polshins, taking Plehbs as mere animals living solely for their amusement, save on Earth.

AND in the hall, furious work was going forward. Nearly twenty of the electron-wave visors were set up within three days, the stamped parts coming out in a steady stream now. The force of permanent dwellers in Mahtan increased now to nearly two hundred and fifty, even the Polshins beginning to notice a slight difference in the city, were working at furious speed. Smaller, simpler clock-drives worked nine of these wave-visors. Nine of these machines were in constant operation observing on the other nine planets, and the great machine was examining the satellite worlds, which it alone could follow. Recording cameras took down everything seen.

The other machines, operated constantly day and night, were observing things on Earth. Five of them observed in N'Yak, the other six were trained on Shkaga, San Franco, Washton, Felfya, and St. Loui.

Swiftly now the campaign with the city was gaining. And now new dies were being cut, dies to make the projection apparatus Bruce had mentioned. In every city men were being chosen, without their even being aware of the examinations, for the local leaders.

Bosn, Felfya, Shkaga, and Washton would be the cities where the first starts would be made. These cities were within the possible range of Bruce's projector, here he would be able to reach out and speak to the men, the personnel, which directors chose.

And Bruce worked constantly at his other problems. Still he had merely begun. They had communication—but not material communication. Time and time again he had tried to make the apparatus transmit the entire piece of matter it viewed. Time and time again—on the tiniest particles—he had failed. When he reached the half-transmitted point, instantaneously some terrific force seemed to wrench all space with unutterable violence. Terrific flaming arcs played momentarily over his apparatus—and it fused in ruins.

So Bruce worked on something else.

CHAPTER SIX

"I AM going to try the new device, Lora. You have taken all those notes, and have them in a safe place?"

"Yes, but oh, Bruce, why can't I try that for you? You know what has happened even with the little transportation devices. If that succeeds too well—the Earth needs you Bruce, as she never before needed any man."

"And I need my self-respect," Bruce replied grimly. "Just as much as any man ever needed it. The Polshins let others suffer pain and death for their amusement or advantage. I'm not a Polshin. I'd never be able to look a man in the eye if I were afraid to do this, and delegated the danger to someone else."

"Can't you make a robot do the thing for you?"

"Again? Can't I convince you that the difference between a man and an intelligent machine is that a man can do what he wasn't designed to—that a machine, no matter how perfect, can't handle an emergency I haven't prepared it for. And since I've done everything in such a way, I don't expect any emergency; that means that if there is one, any machine I designed would be unable to handle it because it was an unexpected emergency. Now you do as I said, Lora. Take the notes and your own small self to a safe place. Go back to the lab."

Lora turned abruptly and raced away.

Bruce grinned after her. He looked again at the apparatus she had helped him build and set up. She was an excellent assistant. She would know what to do if this did blow up. Bruce chuckled at the thought. If it did, working with a one hundredth milligram charge of lithium metal as he was, it would cause a bit of confusion among the Polshins. Lora did not know why he had picked this particular room on the highest level. That he had gone as far as possible up and away from the Mahtan section of the city, she understood. But why this particular room—?

Omallin's fine palace was directly above this room. If Bruce's experiment was unsuccessful, he would remove Omallin, and half the neighboring territory.

Bruce watched the tubes carefully as they heated, and looked again at his stack of accumulators. The power was not on in this distant section, so he had brought his stored power with him. Under the present current drain they'd give out in about three minutes more. It would certainly be embarrassing to go back to Lora and tell her he hadn't even been able to try the thing because he hadn't calculated the power factors right. She'd never trust him afterward.

Bruce jumped as a meter needle rose suddenly and steadily. The electron current had started.

"Well—it's been a nice time, anyway," he laughed. He pushed the control over steadily. Something strained violently. Abruptly, from the small open coil on the table before him, something beautiful and violet and shining sprang like a burning globe. For a billionth part of a second it lasted, perhaps, then, it relapsed suddenly as a mighty tongue of lightning struck down from the granite rock. It struck with a terrible roar, and the apparatus fused in a blinding, incandescent mass, beneath the terrific assault. A roar of awful sound crashed out. Then instantly from the fused apparatus another mighty tongue of electric flame smashed out with equal and opposite titanic power. The rock wall fused, and a great soft drop of liquid rock slipped silently down upon the floor. A cavity two feet deep remained.

But Bruce did not see it. He was motionless and unconscious on the rocky floor.

IT was some fifteen minutes later that Lora and the rescuing men reached him. They were breathless and panting from much running. One of the medically trained men was first to reach him. In an instant he had an electro-stethoscope microphone on his chest. The room echoed abruptly to the powerful, even thump-thump-thump-thump of Bruce's heart. There was a soft, gentle swish of breathing.

"Ah—" Lora darted forward, took a single glance at the wrecked apparatus, a second glance at the recording instruments that had been put on the other side of the room. "Momentary, very short waves. He may be badly burned by them. Now hurry. Jak, Mark, Bob and Pol, take him, and hurry away. Tom and Ban, you take these instruments, and be careful with them. Mal, you take the asbestos things, and scoop up that mess. Now look sharp, the Polshins will be here in a moment. I know why he took this room now—it's right under Omallin's place. I'll bet that electric field turned Omallin inside out when it hit him. He'll be searching down here in half an hour."

Three minutes later, the room was bare. Only the red-hot glowing stone attested to the sudden release of energies stolen from the heart of a sun.

Bruce came to in the laboratory. On the bench was the fused apparatus, cool now. Lora was bending over it, making notes. A tube of liquid carbon dioxide told how she had cooled it, without damaging the sensitive bits that might remain.

"Lora—you watched—the telectroscope?"

"Naturally, Bruce," she snapped. She was still tense, and her nerves unsteady. She had watched, and her heart had contracted once, and stayed just that way, a tense hard lump in her chest till she heard the thump-thump-thump in the doctor's electro-stethescope. She was still nervous—and angry in consequence. "You passed out, and I thought you were dead. Did you see it?"

"No," replied Bruce ruefully. "Only the violet glow."

"That was cosmic ray energy. Lucky it was so hard a radiation. It passed through you like light through glass. Went through so easily, it didn't burn you much. Lasted an infinitesimal time, anyway. But immediately after that, the lightning started. First one bolt from the wall to the apparatus, then the wrecked apparatus replied in kind."

"Kind of it," smiled the scientist. "It let out all that energy in two doses instead of one."

"Think again, Bruce. Wait till you come around. And tell me what you expected, anyway?"

"I wasn't sure, but sort of had a hunch it would be electricity."

"It was—an electric field. It was positive, under the conditions you set up, and it built up to about a million volts instantaneously. Then the wall sent a collection of electrons to neutralize it. They did, and when the last of the matter was used, they were left as a negative charge of a million volts—and went home again."

Bruce sat up slowly. "Why Lora—I didn't think it of you... You are hereby graduated to a first-class independent experimenter. I had no idea you'd found time for so much studying."

Lora felt her heart sink gradually downward, till the touch at the soles of her shoes arrested its progress. Bruce meant it. She would be promoted to an independent investigator's rank. No more work with Bruce. No more even touching his hands at work. No more—

"I couldn't help it with you giving me lectures every time you dropped a bolt. Anyway, you need a nurse. If you expected an electric field, oh Bruce, why didn't you use those brains of yours and put in a discharge point?"

"Unexpected emergency," grinned Bruce. "I had a number four-ought conductor. I expected currents, not lightning bolts."

"A machine could have done a lot better than you did," scolded the girl. Her face was beginning to feel warm again, so she knew the blood must have come back now. She turned from the apparatus, and looked toward Bruce once more.

"All right, girl. I'm clear licked. You can start right now investigating machines to test machines if you want to."

"I'll finish this job first," she said. She'd meant to speak firmly, and a bit sarcastically, but she realized as it sounded, it was more like a plea.

"ALL good. Then we'll start right now making another one—because, Lora, that machine *successfully released all the energy of the matter it worked on!*"

They started another machine, but Bruce realized now what sort of thing he had to deal with. Unlike atomic burners, with their constant streams of electrons at one plate, and protons at the other, uniting to produce tremendous currents of electric power and hydrogen gas, he would get from his machine all the energy of the destroyed matter.

"The waves of the atoms—they aren't real waves—just something that can be expressed by the same sort of formula a wave is expressed by—are all turned one way or the other, with the result that a space-curvature results. I expected a positive electric field then I could as easily have gotten any of the other space-strain energy fields either magnetic, north or south, or gravitational, *plus* or *minus*. In the new machine, I'm going to use a powerful accumulator-device. The positive field will be created momentarily by the release of a tiny bit of energy. This will draw a tremendous negative charge. Then the field will collapse, and the result is a free negative charge, which will seek neutralization. It will yield directly an alternating current of whatever frequency I want. And whatever power I want.

"I can even use this to create directly the momentum waves we discovered.

"And Lora—Lora, with this I can build a tiny hundred-man scout-ship that can yield a hundred billion horsepower— *and never overheat because an electric field is one hundred percent efficient.*"

Bruce was overconfident. He built his apparatus. He tested it, and the tiny thing, no more than three by three by two feet, yielded three million horsepower—and fused the conductors that conducted the current. His electric fields were one hundred percent efficient, but his conductors weren't. Never before had conductors been called on to handle such powers, and still be small conductors. Somehow he must find a conductor that was as efficient as his material-energy engine.

SO—Lora was given the job of investigation, while Bruce began work on some small ships. Two-man ships. They were powered by small models of the material-energy device. Four by four by three they were, because no smaller machine could contain the huge conductors he needed to carry the power. But there were two other material-energy engines aboard. One created the momentum wave, releasing its energy directly, without conductors, in this way. It could have generated at nearly fifty billion horsepower. The other created the anti-gravity field.

The work was needed now, N'yak was nearly unified in the Freedom movement. Slowly the Polshins were becoming aware of something unusual. More and more the Polshins guards really looked around, as they wandered through the streets, really noticed the sullen looks they received. This must have been strange to them. Before, they had been as inevitable as death or taxes in the Old Days. They had been accepted in much the same spirit as those two visitations.

Their shock-rods came more and more into evidence. Strangely the Mating Office was almost deserted now. Only Grays, and an occasional Green couple wandered in.

All the Blues, and most of the Greens had joined the Freedom movement, and there was a tense air of waiting among them. By cosmetics and skillful stage-tricks learned in books, the beautiful women were making themselves ugly. By tricks they made themselves inconspicuous, and with the new, slightly worried air of the Polshins, no more Plehb girls disappeared from their homes.

Just as the new scout-machines, the fleet of six, reached half completion, Don Wade called Bruce. The secret of the isolation of Earth had been learned.

Interplanetary Union Hall at Mars Center had been located. It had been explored, the nine rooms of the Nine planets investigated. A tenth room, with a great seal across it stood in its place. The door was marked "Earth" and below it was the legend:

"I, John Montgommery, have sealed this door in the year 2654. It is not to be opened save by the combined order of the Ten Planets, and then only when Earth, the third planet, shall have again won her place among the Councils of the Planets, and shall have redeemed herself by the re-arising of intelligence among her people."

Don Wade directed the focus to the room within. It was a great room, with a board, long table, and large comfortable chairs. There were books and maps lining the walls. And dust covering all. Dust a quarter of an inch thick lay undisturbed everywhere. At one end of the room, carved in heavy, thick gold, was a great metal plaque. A bas-relief of Earth, with a tiny spaceship leaving her at the top, and below a graven inscription. It was the full text of John Montgommery's farewell to Earth.

Slowly Bruce read it over. Then he nodded slowly. "He was right, Don. That John Montgommery, speaking just about seven centuries ago saw what was coming. The Polshins must have overcome those semi-Plehbs soon after. That is why the libraries were closed, all civilization seemed to stop suddenly. For the last two centuries Earth's civilization had really been maintained by the work of the Planets. Without them dragging her up, Earth fell back instantly to this savage feudalism of vicious pleasure for the Polshins and victims' toil for the stupid, brainless Plehbs.

"Intelligence has arisen again, Don. And today we could go to Mars and redeem Earth. We have the ship—or will have it—within two weeks. The electrovisor here alone would fulfill Montgommery's condition and with material energy—"

"THEN we shall," Don cried. "With the Interplanetary forces behind us, we can wipe out the Polshins in a day."

"That is not what John Montgommery meant," said Bruce shaking his head gravely. "He meant that all the people of Earth should be rejuvenated. We must break the bonds ourselves. We have done only half the work so far.

"We will not go until we can lay down as our claim to redemption, both the inventions and the overthrow of the vicious order that exists. What would Mars reply to such frightful scenes as we picked up that first night we demonstrated the machine? While our women are still being beaten to death by Polshins, we cannot claim redemption.

"This offers only one hope. When we have done this, and have overthrown the Polshins, we will have redeemed the pledge. Then we can have competent teachers from the Planets. In a day we will have the benefits of a civilization we would be able to gain only through many years of teaching and working.

"Until then—we have a titanic task to work out. Your staff has selected the leaders in the other cities?"

"Yes," Don nodded. "I see you're right. And we have the men selected. When will you begin projections?"

"I will begin the day the ships are finished. I think our best plan will be to reach these men by projection, warn them of what we have, and then lead them to some spot in their own Deserted Corridors, and arrange to meet them there."

"We should have more men working here with us permanently. This tiny force is hard put to do more than maintain themselves, let alone all the construction work we require."

"Not another man may we take. Already the Polshin Guards are so suspicious that we cannot afford it. And you know it."

"I have been distributing those little sets you designed," Don sighed. "The men have been able to take them home and conceal them. I have given all the delegates sets, and some of the best of the other men and women. They are holding small meetings in homes now and watching us, and people in other cities with them. Particularly are they showing scenes in Old Mahtan where we have the Old Days living again. That naturally interests them most." Don smiled slightly. "But some of them have begun asking if there is any way to stop these machines. They fear for their privacy eventually."

Bruce burst out laughing. "A thought—a thought the scientist had overlooked. Yes—privacy. I can stop them. A small machine something of the same nature as the projector will instantly warn of the thing, but it will take a bit of work to design a machine to stop it altogether. I think I can do it though, eventually."

CHAPTER SEVEN

"THAT will do," said Bruce. A tall, straight man, with just a touch of gray sat in a sturdy comfortable chair on the stage of the big machine. He seemed unaware of them, bent in deep concentration over his book.

"This is Wil Carny, of Boston. He is a Class A Plehb, a first degree Master of Meks. He is thirty-two years old, a man well liked, and in every way a fine man for the purpose he is to serve," explained Don Wade to the audience grouped about. "He is mated, and has a son, twelve years of age, already a class C apprentice of Meks. Bruce Lawry is to be projected. His voice will be sent first."

Bruce stepped forward. "Wil Carney," he said softly. The seated man started slightly. "Wil Carny, Master of Meks, listen carefully to me. In a moment I will make myself visible. I was a Class A Plehb of the city of N'yak, a master of Meks myself. Now I am a scientist of the Freedom League of N'yak." Carny had risen, and was looking intently, half fearfully about him. "I need your help, Carny. You are a Mek. You were reading, I see. Have you read of the televiso system that was used in the Old Days?"

"Yes—" said the man. "Where are you?"

"I am in N'yak now. I am using such a televiso system. I can see you—and now, you can see me."

Suddenly there was an image of Bruce standing beside the image of Carny. Carny started back, and looked sharply at the white-clad figure.

"At least you look no Polshin," he smiled at length. "Can one so immaterial be seated? If so,—" he waved at the chair.

Bruce smiled. "My advisers have chosen well. You are a man, Wil Carny. Surely I would have been worried by so inexplicable an appearance. I cannot sit in your chair—for I am two hundred miles away. Do you know of the Old Days when men knew more? When they knew why atomic burners worked, and could design them? Do you know of the days when there were no Polshins? I have, with my vision machine, watched your Polshins there in Bosn. They are no worse, nor better than ours in N'yak. They have taken your women. Our machines have shown us what treatment they have received from those Polshins.

"In N'yak we have sought, and found a way to freedom. Not only for us, but for the Plehbs of every city.

"You have visited the Deserted Corridors of your cities have you not? Go to them, and I or my friend will lead you. In half an hour, I will join you there in the body. And I will bring you to N'yak here for a short time. You have still eleven hours of freedom. Will you come?"

"I will come," nodded the older man. Bruce's image faded away. The stage cleared.

It was night, dark on the Surface they knew. But never had one of the ships been tried outside, only in the corridors and Cubes below, and then cautiously. Now Bruce entered the tiny fifteen-foot metal thing, and placed himself at the controls. Gently it lifted. Four hundred men and women waved silently to him as the tiny ship turned, and sped down the corridor, and out of sight. A rim of light preceded it down the dim rocky walls. It disappeared.

Cautiously Bruce drove on. He rose vertically toward the Surface. The tube ended, he knew, in a great metal lock. For centuries these locks had been untouched. But just that day a crew of men had gone there, tested them, oiled them—but not opened them. Bruce sent a brilliant pencil of light on the photocell and waited breathlessly. Outside he knew the Polshins had left them unattended till dirt and rubbish had overgrown them. A crew of men would visit them after he was through for the last time, and cover them again with dirt and rubbish. Later they would make their own smaller lock—a hidden one.

The lock groaned—and opened. Bruce's tiny ship darted up straight into the sky, lightless, soundless. At an altitude of ten miles he leveled off, and shot toward Bosn. Over dark terrain, lighted only by the faint stars and a crescent moon, the ship sped northward. At a speed of nearly a thousand miles an hour, he hovered over Bosn in fifteen minutes. There were lights below, the great illuminated pleasure palaces of the Polshins. Skillfully, as noiseless as a bat, the ship dropped. Here Nature had favored the Plehbs. The lock was unexposed, rocky land, the bare metal showing. No crew need recover it. That was one reason Bosn had been chosen for the first contact.

AT Bruce's signal, the great metal disc swung aside, its century-old bearings groaning faintly. They had built well, when seven centuries before, that lock-door had been made.

The ship dropped through the opening. Starlight sifted down the tube lightless for ages. The ship turned at the third level, and traveled for nearly three miles horizontally. Then, in a great, ruined Cube it halted.

A Cube lightless, and rubbish-floored. Bruce turned to his telectroscope, and sought Wil Carny. He was not in his room, but Bruce quickly located the field of another telectroscope, and found Carny halfway to the Cube already. Patiently he waited.

Half an hour later Wil Carny was shaking hands with him. His eyes were deep and intent as he gazed at the man and the ship. "In this we go to N'yak?" he asked.

"Right," Bruce nodded. "There you will meet the others, and see the machines—and see what Earth was in the Old Days."

In silence disturbed only by the soft, faint whispering of rushing air, the ship slipped down the corridors, and up the tube, out the lock and into the clear, starlit night. Carny gasped at the beauty of the scene. Never had this man been on the surface at night before, never had he seen the beauty of a star-strewn sky, or the silvery moon. Below, endless, broad gardens stretched, soft-lighted with the silver-rose of the glow-tubes. Myriad lights twinkled in the wavelets of Charles River basin on little pleasure boats from fairyland. Two miles below the hovering ship, the whole scene seemed an artists epitomisation of beauty.

Bruce started the telectroscope, and figures of men and women moved on its stage. A boat with colored lights moved slowly across the tiny pool of the stage, then a pier, then a flower-filled garden.

Then another scene. Polshins and a Plehb slave-girl. One of the Polshins was holding a robe, the others short whips. In vain the girl was trying to reach that robe, the whips cutting at her when she paused, or when she came near the robe.

Carny's face went white and tense. His eyes flamed with sudden anger. Gradually his face relaxed as Bruce cut the scene. Knowing where to look, they could see the circle and the figures on a flower-boardered lawn, two miles below. Wistfully Carny looked down.

"Your freedom movement is needed Bruce Lawry, I suppose—" he looked at Bruce thoughtfully.

"No," said Bruce. "Nothing. It is not the first time I have seen such things. I have had to console myself with the poor thought, that shortly it will be ended. I fear only one thing in our movement, Carny. The Plehbs will have a very strong, and very natural tendency to do just such things to Polshins, as Polshins have done to them.

"THAT is what happened in old Russia. The Nobles, some of them, ground down the peasants as cruelly as the Polshins have treated us. When the peasants rose—it was quite natural that they should treat the Nobles so. You have not read of that, probably. The peasants were strange, yet human. They rose, because the Nobles had judged not the man, but his ancestors, and then the peasants gained power and they judged not the man, but the man's ancestors. I fear this freedom movement may tend to the same thing, later.

"You do not know of the Pledge of the Planets. If we institute a system as brutal, as vicious as the present one, merely reversed, Earth will no more have redeemed the Pledge, than she has now.

"You must remember this in the things you will see. It will be very hard, it is hard for us, even the leaders who should be better. You will meet Don Wade." Briefly Bruce outlined the story of Dot Steel, and Don Wade.

"The ancients said of Helen of Troy, that hers was the face that launched a thousand ships. Dot Steel's was the face that launched a million men. Don Wade is bitter. You will, we hope, lead Bosn to the new Freedom, but you must remember always that it is to be a new freedom for *all*— Polshin and Plehb alike. That is a task harder than gaining freedom. We will not, I know, gain it at once. Interplanetary has pledged to help Earth in finishing the settlement of her problems, and we will have to call on them for that. But even so, that the Polshins will suffer during those first few years an oppression nearly as severe as that we suffer now, will perhaps be best for all. For they must learn that others have rights and powers, and the Plehbs must learn to aid his fallen enemy to rise.

"You will soon be there. We are within miles of the lock now, in a few minutes we will enter. Remember this, when you see what you shall see."

The crowd was waiting in the hall as silently patient as when Bruce had left. Wade was the first to shake Carny's hand. "This means more to Earth than you yet know, Carny," he said. "For the first time in seven centuries, the peoples of two cities are in direct communication. Not the Polshins, but the people."

Slowly the crowd moved away toward the restored section of Mahtan. In wonderment Carny looked about him. The crowd had been well disciplined for this occasion, there was no grouping, but free movement along the moving walks, through the lighted shops, and into the theaters. Despite their strong desire to crowd about this man, this man from a city as distant to them as Mars had been to Caesar, they spread out, and brought to Mahtan again that semblance of life. People moved along, passed lighted shop-windows that displayed goods and advertisements of products that had not been manufactured for seven hundred years. The whole section had been made up from photographs seven centuries old.

IN Freedom Hall Carny saw the great telectroscope that had been set up.

"First," said Wade, "we want you to see the Pledge of the Planets." Bruce began operating the machine, and as Mars appeared as a great ball, slowly turning, slowly growing larger,

Wade told Carny briefly and concisely what the situation had been seven hundred years before—and since.

Interplanetary Hall appeared, grew, and they were inside it. Swiftly Wade finished his explanation as the great golden Plaque appeared. The hall was utterly silent as Carny read the words of Montgommery on the Metal Surface.

"The man was a prophet," he sighed at length. "Earth is ready again, I think, to ask the help of the Planets. But as Bruce has said, first we must free ourselves. I will do what I can. It will take a long time."

"Not so long, Carny. We have done a great deal of preliminary work for you, by telectroscope. We have found libraries, and laboratories, hospitals and universities, meeting places and machine shops. We will give you electroscopes, smaller than this machine, but capable of seeing anything on any primary satellite. Fifty of our trained men and women will go to Bosn with you tonight, and by tomorrow night you can have the Bosn organization started, for, by telelectroscope and your personal contacts, we can cover fully a hundred before tomorrow night. And already we have investigated in that way over a half-thousand of the Class A Plehbs in Bosn. They will essentially be the nucleus of your organization.

"We must act rapidly, for, when we strike, we must strike over all the country, and already the Polshins here are beginning to feel the tension. We can spare you no more than fifty of our people, for there is much work to be done here, and of our city of three hundred and fifty thousand, not more than three hundred and fifty can be permanently on our staff here without the Polshins missing them. You, with your three hundred thousand people, must develop an equal staff. To help you, we suggest that many of your people be brought here where our facilities are better, where they can work beside our trained men and learn. But—it is an enormous task. Will you undertake it?"

Carny's face crinkled slowly into a smile. "You investigated me, you said? Your judgement is good, I think, Don Wade. You know what my answer must be. I will. I will, and I will do my best."

CHAPTER EIGHT

A FLEET of twelve tiny ships made the trip to Bosn. Then they returned, for more people, more goods, and more machines. Swiftly, they shuttled back and forth through the black of night, and when dawn at last came on the world of the Surface, material energy engines, telectroscopes, and foods had been carried. And most of all, a staff of fifty trained workers. Technicians had connected in the long-deserted circuits of the corridor lights the tiny but powerful material energy power plants. Lights glowed brightly, and the whole section was lighted again. All the day men and women labored, labored as only a lifetime of labor can teach men to work. When night came again the chosen section of Bosn, the Bluill district, was cleared of rubbish. Windows were lighted again, a theater was open for the reel-plays, shop windows displayed goods, bright, attractive goods. The moving ways moved again, men and women rode on them. The Bluill district seemed again to live. And the Bluill Central Hall was clean and lighted, and on its stage was one of the big telectroscopes, mounted and ready for operation.

The manufactories weren't opened here yet, but foods, goods, a thousand things the luxury-starved Plehbs wanted had been brought from N'yak. Wade had learned well his psychology.

Nearly a hundred men and women of Bosn came that first night. Men and women known personally to everyone of the fifty technicians from N'yak, for they had met them, lived with them, by telectroscope. Carny led the first group, and even he halted in amazement as he reached the rejuvenated district. Last night he had passed this way—a dark, rubbish-heaped area. And now—

Eagerly the hundred were taken in charge. They looked, they wondered. They listened, and began to understand. Then the telectroscope functioned and first they saw Mars—Mars, of the smiling, carefree crowds. Thick crowds of gaily dressed men and women were there in the bright, golden sunlight. It was Mars of the towering graceful, air-washed buildings, glistening multicolored in the sunlight.

Then they saw beautiful sun-lit gardens of the Polshins in San Francisco. They saw the soft-lighted gardens above Bosn. But another operator had been searching; the machine on the stage picked up what he had found—Polshins being amused, a Plehb-slave girl moaning on the ground. A low muttering ripple of sound ran through the audience.

The scene faded, and N'yak appeared on the stage, a scene in Freedom Hall. The audience was gathered there, and on the Freedom Hall stage appeared the scene in this very Hall in Bosn. The six thousand gathered in N'yak rose suddenly, a roaring cheer rang out from the speaker, a hand waved—Spontaneously, the Bosn people responded.

In that instant the friendship, the solidified feeling of real, close kinship with those people they had never seen, those people in the far, far distant city of N'yak, sprang up full grown.

Hours later the Bosn crowd spread out, seeking their way homeward. Everyone was a missionary now, the New Freedom, conditions were so vastly different. The leaders were so different. There was an Ams, a Lozh and a Kabt listed on the rolls of the Polshins—contractions, modifications of names that had stood for the finest things in the Old Freedom.

IN N'yak work went on, harder than ever before. There were fewer trained hands now, and more unskilled workers from Bosn. But it was easier too, for the giant of Material Energy stood at their shoulders, pushing as they willed, lifting at their gesture. And Bruce had found the disintegrating machine. Tiny, ultra-microscopic bombs, scarcely more than large ions, were shot out against the rock or metal to be destroyed, and those particles released their energy of existence as an electric field of such unimaginable density, that mere atoms caught up in them were strained beyond the strength of any possible electric structure. Abruptly, they collapsed, collapsed to electron and proton, to neutron and positron. No nucleus was left even, the very heart of the atoms was ripped to shreds. Free hydrogen was left over, the atoms themselves were decomposed. Free hydrogen gas rose from the working machine, and burned blue and pale in the glow of the lights. Otherwise there was little display, no more sound than a strange, eerie whispering of atomic death. All the energy was absorbed in breaking the atoms, the machine was efficient to almost complete silence.

Modified atomic burners had been able to transmute certain elements partly into certain other elements under certain conditions. This machine disintegrated the "certains" as completely as the rock. In a day, a score of men were released from the transmutation work, for a single material energy disintegrator could first shatter the atoms to gas, then whirl the shattered parts into whatever figuration was desired. The raw materials, iron and aluminum, carbon and sulfur, for foods and machines, became plentiful. And now the building of the greater ships, the battleships of the Freedom

Movement, was undertaken. The "Freedom" ships were started before their plans were finished.

Three weeks after the first crew went to Bosn, they returned, and in their stead went the men who had been trained in N'yak. Bosn had established her own government. A second group was sent out, not technicians now, but teachers, a bare half-dozen men and women. The libraries scattered about Bosn had been moved bodily to the Bluill Central, and day and night three hundred studied as intently as it was possible for humans to study, humans trained to work. By night, a thousand more were added to the roll of students. And regular meetings were being held, constantly growing meetings. Telectroscope theaters showed the planets and Earth as they were at the moment; reel-theaters showed Earth as it had been in the Old Days.

The day the Bosn crew returned to N'yak, the first contact was made with Felfya. Jon Roger had been chosen here, and entrance was effected by means of the disintegrator working under complete coverage. All one night a crew of fifty men had to work, and half the next night before the necessary locks had been bored, and carefully hidden. Then Jon Roger was contacted, and brought to N'yak, saw the scenes the telectroscope displayed, scenes from Mars, and from Bosn. And scenes in a Polshin garden above Felfya itself.

When he went back a crew of fifty technicians went with him. Two weeks later there was a crew of thirty Bosn men and women working in Felfya to hasten the work.

Meetings in N'yak were restricted, now that nearly all the members had the tiny telectroscopes. N'yak's main section must be given some air of normalcy. The Polshins were beginning to conduct occasional searches. Half-hearted—inexpert—but searches. More and more the crew in the Mahtan section saw the true size of their task. Yet Bosn and Felfya were barely able to maintain themselves, so much of their energies were spent in learning, desperately trying to catch up with N'yak, and pull their own share of the load.

A steady traffic of noiseless, lightless, black ships was maintained, carrying load after load of machines, mainly material energy engines, and small telectroscopes. And now loads were being sent to Felfya. For the party had caught, and spread as swiftly here as in Bosn.

Faster and faster the pace must be. For the Polshins, cruel as they might be by simple inconsideration of any save themselves, were not unintelligent. In N'yak they had begun to re-awaken to the possibility of trouble. Soon there would be troubles at home. The movement must be well rooted elsewhere before this began.

IN three weeks more, Washton was contacted. And a week later, Bosn herself sent out an expedition, for what they may have lacked in training there, they made up for in enthusiasm, determination, and plain human knowledge. It took no skill or technique to interest men in such an obvious cause. The Plehbs were intelligent once more, only the spark of hope, only some indication that the thing existed, was needed to start them trying. N'yak contacted Shkaga for the Bosn crew that went out to take over. And they went in Bosn-made ships. The men of Bosn were skilled workers, the Mek Plehbs there had done the same sort of work the Meks of N'yak had done. They needed only to be shown how. Now Bosn was beginning to manufacture machines. Month succeeded month in bewildering, fast-spreading action. Nearly the entire Blue and Green classes of N'yak had been enrolled, most of Bosn, and Felfya, Shkaga and all three were producing now.

There were other inventors. But none equaled Bruce. Bruce was the one super-genius that must inevitably have arisen, as John Montgommery had predicted.

But Bruce had been able to devote little of his time to his real work. Too much had to be done in the building of the new Freedom. There were elected officers from every city in the Union now, and officers were elected who represented the Union Government. And Bruce had been made President.

It was too great an honor for him to refuse. His personality meant too much to the people. But he had done almost nothing, it seemed to him. Still the "Freedom" remained incomplete.

Finally, he resigned his office. It was a difficult step, one that he thought over for hours before taking. But on the second anniversary of the first beginnings of the Freedom movement, the second anniversary of Dot Steel's loss, he resigned.

CHAPTER NINE

"YOU have carried on my work, Lora. I feel proud of myself. I never knew I was such a good judge of people," he smiled at her. "I am afraid I hadn't thought of this possibility. Do you think it can be done?"

Lora laughed merrily at his smiling face. Bruce was back in the laboratory again. And she was a full-fledged investigator, associated with him as an equal now—anyway, she was not a laboratory assistant. "What do you think I spent my time on it for, Bruce? Certainly it can be done. You tried the directed electric field, and got a 'little where' with it. But your columns of strained space lacked electrons. Pure space-fields won't do some of the things you need, so I tried combining the best features of the two. I think that by putting your column of space through a silver bar conductor, you will get the effect of perfectly free electrons. Since your generator will give only alternating current, this will do as well. For some smaller apparatus, you will still have to use straight metal conductors, but you will need heavy currents for only two things—deflecting the enemy weapons and running certain of your own weapons.

"Most of the enemy weapons are electric in nature—accumulator shells, ball-lightning, ion-streams. I think a straight magnetic field generated by the material engine will stop that."

Rapidly she outlined her plan, watching eagerly the looks of approval Bruce gave to her calculations. Perhaps after all, this was the way. Bruce was not like other men.

But it also was the way to the completion of the "Freedom."

In two weeks of research, Bruce began to see the way to do what they needed, and in a month, the last stage had been reached. The apparatus was being installed in the "Freedom."

Other "Freedom" ships were being built now, in the other cities. The blow would have to come soon. The Polshins of all cities were beginning to worry. The Polshins Council at Washton had discussed the problem with gravity and real thought. The usual amusements were rather half-hearted, for this actual problem to solve—a real decision to make—made the usual social meeting unhappy—and troubled. The tension among the Plehbs had first been noticed in N'yak. Omallin it was, who suggested that he conduct a search, and find out if there were any such thing as a revolution in the air. He couldn't exactly imagine what a revolution might be, but it worried him. It might upset production seriously, a thing that had never happened in his life, nor in the lives of his forefathers for fifteen generations back.

The call went out from N'yak headquarters, and every member of the Movement hid his telectroscope more carefully. Not yet were the conditions right. San Francisco had been added to the Union so recently it was not at all properly equipped. Perhaps, if this search were passed successfully, the pleasure-loving, thoughtless Polshins would decide that it was nothing, and another year even might be gained. Across the deserted belt of the Tropics somewhere were other cities they had not been able to contact, because of the difficulties of projecting images more than 1000 miles. Nor had they reached Europe or Asia. Many cities in North America were still unprepared.

Hurriedly arrangements were made by the N'yakers. This search was to be something such as they had never experienced. The Meks of the city were almost called in to fix up the old televiso system where possible, but Omallin was actually studying the problem. He had found a Plehb girl who could read, and she was reading to him out of the old books and papers of his forefathers. They told of earlier revolutions and precautions taken. Secrecy—thoroughness—those seemed to be the keynotes. So he did not warn the Plehbs by having the televiso system restored. That the Plehbs should know, he realized was a bad move.

The audience of two thousand Plehbs in N'yak Freedom Hall laughed at his decision, and a half million Plehbs, gathered in Freedom Halls over the greater part of be continent, laughed with them, as they watched the scene of Omallin's conference.

But they didn't laugh at a point Omallin had dug out and decided on. The records. The records were to be used to check up. Those deadly records—they, despite all else were accurate as a stock inventory ever had been, for to the Polshins the Plehbs were stock, stock for their use, and these deadly records always had been used. Every Plehb must be in his place, when the check-up was made, every absence accounted for.

HASTILY a council was called. Men and women from Bosn, from Shkaga and from Felphya came in to help, to maintain the Mahtan district. To fill vacancies. For since the Freedom movement started, the Plehbs had not obeyed all the laws. Nearly a score had died, and their deaths had not been properly reported to the Polshin medical officers. For the Freedom doctors were infinitely better. The telectroscope was a diagnostic instrument such as even the men of the Old Days had never had—when the organs of the patient could be examined in action with precision and ease by the doctor. And these doctors had trained themselves from the old, accurate books.

Further, there were three hundred and sixty-two adult members of the permanent staff—and over half had married. Few of these were married according to the records of the Mating Office. They were married here in Mahtan, married, not mated according to the laws of the Polshins. And there were forty-five children.

Hastily men from the other cities took the places of the dead, where needed, women took charge of the children, the couples parted, and went back to the homes of their parents.

The search day found everything normal on the surface— and a terrific tension beneath the surface. A tension far greater than there ever had been before. Polshin guards appeared everywhere, Polshins from other cities. At that Bruce and Don felt their hearts drop. Polshin Guards from other cities, Polshins from Bosn, from Felfya, from Shkaga... There were men and women, who came from those cities, here taking the places of dead. The chance was slight—but it existed.

Restlessly Bruce paced the stonewalled, bare apartment of his father. A tiny signal hidden in a button of his blue and gold Master Mek suit glowed dully twice. The Polshin squad was coming down this corridor now. The men in Mahtan were warning him. There would be no telectroscopes to find. They were all back in Mahtan now. But nearly every member wore one of the tiny detector buttons that would warn him when the Polshins approached.

There was a rapid winking of his button, then it went out all together. The voices of Polshins, sharp and domineering, came up the stair-tube from below as it winked out.

"Apartments A, B, and C, Landun. D, E, and F, Morly, and—"

Bruce seated himself stolidly in his chair. His father came in from the other room, and seated himself. He had a tattered, broken book, and slowly, his finger on the page, he began to read it.

He raised his keen eyes slowly to his son. "Bruce," he said, "we are frightened. Badly so. But we must do something, and we are stupid. So I read. And you sit there very stupidly. Your face is tense and white. There is anger and intelligence in your eyes. There is pride and self-respect in your shoulders, and the set of your head. Take them out, Bruce."

Softly Bruce laughed. A Polshin threw open the door almost simultaneously. Bruce looked up at him sullenly, his rounded shoulders slightly drawn away.

"UP, Plehbs," snapped the Polshin. Slowly the two men rose, and faced the young Polshin. He came over to them, while a companion stood in the doorway. The second man held a sheaf of records.

"Name, Plehb?" the first demanded sharply, looking at Bruce.

"Bruce Lawry, Polshin Sir."

"Age, and status."

"Thirty-one, and I am a Class A Master Mek, Polshin Sir."

"Check," said the man in the doorway.

"You?" snapped the inquisitor turning to old Jon.

Briefly, obediently, Jon Lawry answered his questions.

"Check," said the man in the door. They entered then, and with quick, but thorough methods, searched the entire bare stone room. There was little chance of concealment here, it seemed. In two minutes they were satisfied, and moved on.

A minute later Bruce's mother came in quietly and sat down. "They were very hurried, and quite bearable," she said quietly. Bruce's button winked twice. The Polshins had left the building.

"Voice—softly," said he quietly into the air.

"Ready, Lawry," answered a soft voice from the air.

"How has the search gone so far?"

"They have found nothing whatsoever. One of the Bosn men was examined by a Bosn Polshin—but the Polshin examining him did not know it. He was not expected a Bosn Plehb here.

"Observer fifty-three reports that Don Wade is being examined. A Shkaga Polshin. Another pair has finished and is coming—God—" suddenly the voice was tense with horror, "—*they're fighting!* Don attacked the new Polshin instantly. Don Wade—is dead. Shock-rod. He attacked the Polshin with a chair. His brains ate spattered all over the room. I can't understand—I can't understand—"

"Pick up that scene and project it here, instantly," snapped Bruce, something tight in his throat.

"Right, Lawry. A moment."

Abruptly, in mid-air, the scene appeared, then sound. A dozen Polshin guards had come at the call. On the floor lay a sprawled, bleeding figure, the scarlet cloak spotted horribly with a grayish-red substance. Beside him lay another inert figure, its fingers clasped tightly about the metal bars of a chair, a chair covered with the stain that spotted the dead Polshin's cloak.

There was not enough of the Polshin's face left to recognize. An angry, snarling grumble of conversation drowned out individual voices. "Which," demanded Bruce, "was the second of the pair that came in together?"

An enormous finger touched one of the miniature figures in the scene, and the figure swayed. "This," replied the voice of the operator.

"It is the second of the Polshin Guards in the Mating Office that day," said Bruce softly. "It is the man who saved Don's life that day. The dead Polshin is the one Don struck, I am sure."

"I've seen him—I've seen him before" said a voice from the tiny scene. The Polshin the finger had pointed out was speaking. The others stared at him. "I know! I saw him in the Mating Office two years and more ago. His woman was taken just as he was about to mate with her—Omallin... We were ordered to take her out, this Plehb struck Tomsun then. He must have remembered—killed him today."

"HE couldn't stand the sight of that man, I guess," said Bruce softly. "He should not have done that—not only for himself, but for Freedom. We needed him too badly."

But Bruce wondered as he said it, if, perhaps, it were not best thus. Don would not have been contented merely with freedom for the Plehbs. And Don had won, for what he had started, lived, though he died. The Freedom Movement would go on. He had endangered it by that act, though, for the Polshins were angry now, furious. They would be harsh—but put it down largely to a two-year-old grievance.

In the end it might even aid in discouraging further searches.

"How are they treating our women?" Bruce asked at last.

"Fairly well. The prettiest have used all their art to make themselves unattractive. And the Polshins are very intent. They feel the seriousness of this. They will come back though—at least some have promised themselves they would."

"That is what I fear most," admitted Bruce. "Get in touch now with Manning. He will be president now that Wade is dead. Tell him what has happened, do as he says, of course. And let me know from time to time how things are going.

"It's hard to realize—Wade dead."

CHAPTER TEN

"MARY has been reading some of the old records to me," said Omallin pompously to his council, "and in the Old Days, my forefathers got some aid from certain of the Plehbs. He picked certain of those who seemed to have sense, or the dim beginnings of it, and found that by offering them certain advantages, they would furnish him with information regarding the activities of the other Plehbs.

"I wonder if we might not try the same system."

The members of the council looked disgusted. Have dealings with a Plehb—offer something in return for a favor from a Plehb?

Bruce, watching the images in the telectroscope, was not so disgusted with this plan. There were still certain Plehbs who had not been invited to join the Freedom party, either because of their stupidity, as in the case of most of those who had risen no higher than the Gray class, or because of their characters. And those refused because of their characters, were just the ones the Polshins would want. There were some seven thousand of them—and the permanent crew could not possibly keep so many under constant supervision by telectroscope. It was a physical impossibility.

"The idea," said Vanilt, "is preposterous. Associating with and asking favors of Plehbs."

"Our forefathers did it," Omallin replied. "Besides, it might furnish us much amusement, listening to the tales of the Plehbs."

"What reward can we offer them?" asked Morn unpleasantly.

Omallin laughed. "Our fathers solved that. Plehb girls. They chose the ones who could not win wives—and it worked very well."

"Hmm—but there seems to be a great dearth of Plehb women as it is. I have not seen a really beautiful one in two years."

But before the council broke up, the thing had been decided on. The Polshin Guard members were to select the ones needed. They were to do it secretly. And the system to be used was one so cleverly worked out, that not even with the aid of the telectroscope would all the members of the Polshin spy-ring be detected at once. Many of course, would be actual members of the Freedom movement, for they now numbered two hundred and eighty thousand in a city of three hundred and fifty thousand. Inevitably, the Polshin Guards would choose many of these.

That night in the Meeting Hall, Bruce and other officials of the Movement spoke, spoke to an audience of, apparently, less than four hundred, actually to all the Freedom members of the city, watching with their tiny telectroscope machines. Carefully Bruce outlined the dangers, and carefully those who followed him, outlined the defense. Those chosen were invariably to accept. They were to do their best to learn what nonmembers of the Freedom party belonged to the ring.

In a week, the ring began to grow. That week saw the inclusion of Sattl and Dllas into the ring of Union cities. The system of choosing the spies that the Polshins had gotten from the old records, was simple—simply choose enormous numbers of spies, choose so many at once that no counter-spy system could follow all. Many, they realized, would be members of any movement there might be toward revolt, but no two chosen saw each other. They were not visited in offices, but Polshin guards spoke a word or two on the Corridor. And Guards were everywhere since the search and the murder of a Polshin. Over two thousand guards stood about everywhere. During the rest-hours, every single member was watched, but the night hours were rest hours for the Polshins too, and no business was transacted. No clues were dropped, no hints released. The spy ring was completed—and made tight.

AND—the first arrest was made within two weeks. A genuine Freedom Delegate from the fifty-second section. How the spy had learned, how he had communicated his information, even who he was remained an utter mystery. But Mark Rainy was the first victim, and he set the example for others of those who were to be captured. He was arrested at his work, while repairing a slight break in a food-machine. Four Polshin Guards took him, whisked him swiftly to an office somewhere in the Polshin section. It was ten minutes before this could be picked up, and followed, for a messenger had to make his way to the nearest communication station in the outlying Deserted Corridors to signal the information.

They located him finally by following Omallin. Omallin came to that first inquisition, to learn what truth there was in the story a hundred spies had brought in, that there was some movement toward revolt. Rainy was bound now, and as Omallin entered, the questioning began. Not a word would Rainy speak. With a delicate precision, the Polshins applied their shock-rods. Terrible, nerve-wrenching shocks were sent through his body. Rainy said nothing, save to deny that such a movement existed. He was humbly pleading at first. Then stubbornly angry, persisting in his declaration that there was no such movement. Admitted that he went out secretly many nights—could he not visit a friend secretly? Who was the friend? A Plehb did not explain such things.

Then he somehow loosened one of the inexpertly tied bonds. With a grim determination, a stolid decision, he attacked Omallin and before a dozen shock-rods coagulated his nerves into death, he had battered Omallin's fat-swathed hook nose into a bleeding, pulpy spread.

Bruce smiled grimly as the last act of the strange drama on the Freedom Hall stage came to its end. "I am glad to think the Polshins have no Plastic Surgeons such as ours. Omallin will resent that more than any other thing."

A new tenseness and hatred developed among the Plehbs, more virulent even than their hate of the Polshins, and one even harder to express. Somewhere in this city were Plehbs, their own people, who had turned against them.

And with the building up of the spy ring, came a still greater threat. Omallin had to build up another force. He had to gather means of keeping his promise to Plehb spies. A horrible terror gripped the heart of every girl, every mother and every father, every brother or sweetheart.

Swiftly the tenseness was building up. Bruce knew that every day brought the inevitable climax nearer. As yet no more girls had been taken, for Omallin was still testing his spies, still uncertain. He believed largely what he wanted to believe, and he did not want to believe and could not believe that actual danger of revolution threatened him.

A second arrest was made, Jim Brady, a member of the Freedom movement. And Jim Brady killed the Polshin who arrested him with his great, work-hardened hands. His powerful fingers fastened on his throat with a grip that drove them through the flesh, and the shock-rod currents only served to bring a *rigor mortis* that locked the dead fingers more tightly yet. The two dead bodies were carried away together, that a surgeon might separate the Plehb and his Polshin victim.

THAT night there was a tenseness among the Polshins as great as among the Plehbs. A Polshin had died, died horribly. There were no skilled morticians to hide the horrible, torn throat, and the Polshins who had neither suffered injury, nor been called on for the least display of courage in generations, wilted spiritually before that wound. The council was more serious than ever it had been before. And there was little amusement in the gardens of the Polshins that night. Polshins looked on their Plehb slave-girls and saw burning in their eyes a deep, smoldering hate. There was a new suppleness in them, the soft suppleness of a snake as it creeps upon its victim, for everyone of those Plehb girls knew now of the Freedom movement, and every one knew that a Plehb had torn the throat out of a Polshin.

By dawn the Polshins were inspecting old atomic cruisers, looking again at the old ion-guns that had swept death through a thousand corridors in past years. And by dawn they knew that a half-dozen Plehb girls had died, died attacking the Polshins that came to them. One had swung a chair, the heaviest her muscles could wield, and sent the man to the hospital with a fractured skull. He was dead by noon. Two had tried to emulate Jim Brady, and left deep scars on the throats of the men they attacked. Only their lack of strength had made the wound painful instead of fatal. And one, swimming in a pool, had wrapped her arms around a Polshin, and drowned with him. Two more had been stopped in time. There was no doubt about the Freedom movement now. Every Plehb knew it, and every Polshin. All

N'yak stirred restlessly with it, and Polshins in every other city of the country were suddenly aware of the danger. They too were thinking of making searches.

Omallin ordered another. Bosn and Felfya sent a few Polshin guards. Every Polshin in N'yak would engage in this search. And the spies were contacted throughout the city. In haste, it was done-hurriedly. By noon the search would begin. And the first search party found twenty-three corpses in the first sector they investigated. Spies—spies burned with curious round wounds that had let out life instantly.

The Freedom scientists had found their hand-weapons. Twin pistols, one shooting a stream of electrons, the other a stream of protons. Effective up to fifteen feet, no Polshin would get near enough to use his shock-rod when a man carried these. They had heavier weapons, too, weapons being groomed all that night, great tubes five feet long, mounted on little trucks. In the base was a material-energy engine, an engine that released the colossal energy of matter as an inconceivable, positive electric field. Like the disintegrator, it would tear any atom to sub-atomic fragments—and hurl the protons out with a velocity to two thousand million volts! No insulation would have resisted such a potential, but insulation capable of handling a hundred thousand surrounded the tube, and a smaller projector within the projector shot out a preliminary stream of protons that broke down the air ahead to form a leading path that the titanic discharge followed. First the bolt of protons, then the electrons were released and shot out to follow. What this weapon directed its forces against dissolved into hydrogen gas. No complex, balanced atomic structure could resist that bombardment.

Bosn was starting its search, so they planned at least, in two days. Meanwhile their Guards were loaned to N'yak.

N'yak would reciprocate, of course, when their search came about.

AT noon the groups started out. They had spies' directions now. And every squad carried cosmetic-removing materials. The Mahtan section, in charge of Bosn and Shkaga men and women, watched every step of the progress, while Bruce, in his home, watched what he wanted. The big telectroscope projector would allow two-way communication when needed, and this time every Freedom member had kept, in secret compartments, both their telectroscope apparatus, and the hand-weapons the Freedom scientists had distributed. The compartments hollowed out of the solid rock with disintegrators, in most cases, and hidden behind steel doors, faced with granite.

"They have found the corpses," said a soft voice in Bruce's ear. "They are reporting to Omallin and the Council. Omallin is greatly perturbed." The voice allowed itself a chuckle. "He has ordered that spies be questioned carefully when visited, for any more recent information."

Bruce watched the tiny stage of his own telectroscope. A party of Polshins was investigating Hal Powr, Vice-president of the Union. He smiled as the Polshin guards left Powr and his "mother," a high-ranking Bosn woman who had taken the place of the gentle old lady who had died seven months ago in Mahtan Hospital.

Steadily, and with grim determination the search went on. It was a colossal job to search the one hundred and eight thousand apartments of N'yak. And three guards, the shock-rods at the ready, made each search. Carefully they looked this time. And Bruce trembled at the possibilities, the almost positive certainties that must come of this search. He had hoped for more time. They needed it so vitally. Yet all over the city now, Polshin Guards were looking, and wondering.

Girls, beautiful, fair complexioned, slim, graceful girls were blossoming out suddenly now, whereas in the search made a few short weeks ago, there had been none. Cosmetic trickery would have been a signed admission of membership in the Union, padding that had distorted lithe figures before would have been as bad, for cosmetic removers were being plied with a will, dozens of girls had been forced to prove their clothes had no padding. And Polshins were making mental notes.

"This search makes things impossible, Bruce," said the Voice worriedly. "The Polshins will be back, individually, to demand those girls now. For two years they have found almost none, and the spies—they must be satisfied."

"You may as well send out the word to prepare for the final rebellion," assented Bruce sadly. "We will be hard-pressed. We have four Freedom ships ready here, four in Bosn, three in Felfya, three in Shkaga, and two in each of several other cities. But so many of the new member cities have none, and no proton guns. This night we must distribute the proton-tubes. You will get an immediate vote on this from the other members of the—my button flashes." Abruptly Bruce swung shut the granite-sheathed door of his telectroscope machine's hide-away. He straightened, and turned to the doorway, Polshin voices were snapping tensely below. Bruce waited patiently, humbly and correctly he answered their questions as they were asked, as did his father.

In five minutes they left his apartment again.

And almost instantly, before the door had more than closed, the Voice was back, softly, but infinitely tense. "Bruce—emergency. A spy has reported, and the report was carried directly by telephone, to Omallin. A spy living next to Lora has reported her definitely as a member of the Union, and as one high in the organization. A Polshin party arrested her while you were being examined, and took her away, immediately. She is bound and bound expertly. They are entering Omallin's inquisition room now."

"GOD," said Bruce. Instantly he snapped open the little door, and brought out the telectroscope. In a moment his flying fingers had trained it on Omallin's office, Lora, her hands bound tightly behind her, was being held by two Polshins. She was smiling slightly.

"I've heard you were fat," she said calmly to Omallin. "But I didn't know a human could be so hideous. And that nose!"

Omallin's red face went purple. Then it went white. "Plehb, that being your opinion, I shall make you my slave for a time, after we have learned what we will from you, and then you shall amuse our spies. And then you shall finish paying for that very slowly."

"All three wrong, Omallin. Long before that, someone will finish what Mark Rainy started."

"Hold her," snapped the Polshin, "and no matter what she tries, do not kill her. Tie her to the frame over there." Omallin took off his cloak, and picked up a pliable wire cable, its ends frayed as the two Guards swiftly and efficiently did as he had ordered.

"I will start with ten blows," said Omallin, "and after that, anything you may want to say, I will be glad to listen to." He drew back his arm, and slashed viciously at her. A livid streak came running across her back, and halfway around her body. She jerked conclusively.

"You know the Freedom movement has started, Omallin," she said in a deadly calm voice. "That is all that matters. That, and the fact that you will die inevitably: You personally, Omallin. You yourself will be killed. Not someone else. You will probably kill me here today—but someone else will kill you, Omallin. And—do you know?

Probably a hundred thousand eyes are watching every move you make. And a hundred thousand ears hearing every word you say. And what I say."

"Quiet, lying Plehb." The girl's body jerked to another blow.

"Lying—am I? Then Tom, show them—it does not matter now, for there is nothing they can do. Show them!"

Bruce did not see this. In fact, he had stopped watching almost immediately after the first blow. But Tom Philips did, and Tom Philips at the telectroscope projector spoke into Omallin's ears.

"She might have added, Omallin, that fifty thousand Plehbs are promising themselves individually to kill you."

Omallin's face went whiter than ever before. Furiously he spun around, seeking the source of that voice. But only the white startled faces of the other Polshins greeted him. Suddenly he regained his courage. The ghost voice—but they could do nothing. They had done nothing that was the proof of it.

"Then if all those miserable Plehbs are watching—let them see! And let them remember that I promise this to every Plehb who dares to think of harming a Polshin." Viciously he spun back to Lora. His arm swung up and down. Again. It rose again—and stopped abruptly in mid swing as a giant ten feet tall loomed suddenly, solidly before him. A giant in loose, white clothes trimmed with gold and bright blue.

"STOP," roared the giant, his eyes lambent with anger and hate. "Stop, and out of this room!"

Precipitately the Polshins fled the room, fled it in terror. Only the bound girl remained in the rock-walled room. "Thanks—Tom," she replied. Her head fell forward loosely as the white-clad giant vanished. He had other work. The Polshins would be back in minutes.

Bruce had left his electroscope when the first blow fell. He had slammed the little door shut, and burst out of the apartment on swift feet. In his two hands were the twin bearers of death, which the Freedom scientists had designed, and in his heart was a sudden understanding for Don Wade and his mad murder of the Polshin Guard. Something hot and driving had clutched him, something that seemed to distort everything he saw, that made the Polshin Guard suddenly before him a monster, leering with devil-eyes at him, rather than a semi-stupefied young man. The Polshin fell silently as twin, ravening beams tore into his chest.

That something had made him see more clearly though. He saw Lora's keen, laughing eyes different, and more clearly. He saw suddenly that she was *Lora*, not his keenest, quickest, wisest helper.

He saw a squad of Polshin Guards fall suddenly as the two beams bit into them, and heard the shrilling of their warning whistles stilled as suddenly as they fell. He caught glimpses of the corridors as he raced through them. But most of the time the windows and lighted passages were clouded over by a great fat Polshin in a scarlet suit, his angry white face, and a white back with an angry scarlet stripe.

He realized suddenly that a voice was calling him, the voice. "Bruce—Bruce, for God's sake listen!" He halted suddenly, sliding to an abrupt stop. "Bruce, they stopped. I used the projector at Lora's authority to frighten the coward's away. What shall I do now?"

Suddenly Bruce was cold and sane. Only his viewpoint was changed, all life seemed to have different ends and aims. "Right, Tom. Thanks. Get observers to watch around me for Polshins. I can handle them, but I want to know."

"We've done that. Followed you all the way."

"Good. Send warnings to the other cities with the smaller projectors, at once. This search will end here in short order now, and then use the projectors to gather the people here. Now, send the small ship we have armed with the proton-tubes to me here, at once. Brady's the very best pilot. Send Grant along, we'll need him to treat Lora."

"BRUCE—they came back for Lora just now. The big projector's on them. I'm going over." Another voice came on suddenly. "I'm using the secondary projector. Tom Philips is trying to drive off the Polshins. They've touched his image with shock-rods, and the opposing field shorted the rod so it fused in the Guard's hand. There's a dozen guards, and they won't leave. They've cut Lora down, and are taking her. She's unconscious now, it seems.

"They've got an atomic pleasure-ship in the Corridor, and they're in it now. Taking Lora—Down Corridor F and now, up tube 36. In the open now, above the surface. Taking her—they're taking her to the N'yak Fortress! All the Polshin families are moving in there hurriedly. They're really frightened—Omallin's gone there already, with his crew— Taking Lora into one of the cells— Put her on a couch— Surgeon has been called— Omallin must have different plans now.

"The surgeon's working. Lora's come to her senses. Philips is talking to her now. The surgeon's backed out, scared. The Polshin guards have come back, and they've tied Lora down. Lora says she's all right."

A ship, sixty feet long and ten in diameter appeared just above Bruce. There was a strange quiet in this part of the city, near the Deserted Passages now. The ship dropped lightly, and Bruce jumped in at once. On the stage of the electroscope of the ship was the scene in the cell in the N'yak fortress. Four Polshin guards were binding down Lora with a careful efficiency, paying no attention to the ten-foot figure of Tom Philips standing beside her. Lora was talking.

"—Bruce to start things, I'm afraid, but tell him that if he is going to go anywhere, be sure he can land before he jumps off."

Tom Philips spoke. "Bruce has started things, Lora. He's just been picked up by one of our ships in Corridor F-R. He's watching now on the ship electroscope."

The Polshin guards had finished, and were standing about helplessly now, the scene wavering slightly due to the motion of the ship as it returned to the berth in the Deserted Corridors. Lora smiled faintly.

"That's better—then I can talk to you, Bruce. Remember that for months you have been working out a plan, and that plan is the best that human ingenuity has been able to evolve. Go to it."

A POLSHIN messenger appeared suddenly, and spoke sharply to the leader of the guards in the room. A moment later a second doctor appeared, evidently the first would not come back. This man at once shooed the Polshin Guards out of the room, clapped his palm under Lora's chin, and then put a piece of adhesive across her mouth. Swiftly the doctor set to work, inspecting her wounds and putting *theta*-paste over them. In thirty seconds the *theta*-paste had hardened, and contracted, pulling the edges of the cuts together, meanwhile disinfecting them. He cut the wire bonds the Polshin guard had placed on her, and looked up at the towering figure of Tom Philips.

"Really, you disconcert a worker. Can you see anywhere with that device?"

"From Mercury to Athena. Or don't you know them?"

"I know them," the surgeon nodded. "The Planets. You can actually see so far?"

"Further. We have never really tested it out."

"Through rock and metal. Hmm—wonderful diagnostic instrument, isn't it. You have surgeons, I suppose."

"Better than any of the Polshins know. We have all the books of the Old Days at our disposal—and our surgeons study at the Interplanetary Center on Mars."

The Polshin smiled deprecatingly. "Really, I'm ashamed of my profession here. What must one do to join your new school of medicine?"

"Be a man, a Plehb," snapped Tom Philips.

Bruce, in the ship, called out now.

"No, Philips. Listen to me. The first is right. The second is not indispensable. Tell him that."

"Bruce, our leader," said Philips more calmly, "says that only the first is indispensable."

"Then, perhaps I might learn to qualify. I have often wondered whether some of the people I have met were truly human. Omallin for instance. I'd classify him as belonging to the pig family." The man had turned back to his work now, and had injected something into Lora's arm. "Omallin had some pleasant plans for this young woman. He will be interested when I make my report. That was a fifty-milligram injection of *delta*-morphium. Do your men know it?"

"It will put her to sleep, and keep her unconscious for two full days," said Dr. Grant in Bruce's ear. "Nothing will waken her save certain of the new drugs developed in Mars Central. They do not have any."

Philips relayed Grant's report. "Ah, you are indeed ahead of us. Unfortunately—or should I say fortunately—we know of nothing, which will disturb the slumbers of the patient. She ought to drop off in five minutes—"

A SQUADRON of Polshin Guards came down the corridor, with Omallin fearfully following behind. The doctor looked out at them annoyed. "I'm working with my patient," he said, "and it isn't necessary for you to disturb her now, is it?"

"Yes," Omallin growled. "It is. I wish you'd get that thing," pointing to the looming Philips, "out of the way."

"He's quite harmless, so far as I can see. But can't you wait a few minutes? I have given the girl some injections."

"No. We have to find out where that thing is operating from. A Plehb in the city ran wild and killed no less than eleven Polshins. He simply disappeared—at least we can find no one who admits seeing him go anywhere."

Tom Philips suddenly vanished from the room, and Bruce Lawry's image appeared. "He's here, Polshin Coward," said Bruce gently. "Quite safe, thank you. Much safer than you are."

Omallin spun sharply to look at the new image. Angrily he roared at it. "Before I'm through with you and your ilk, you'll learn better than to insult a Polshin!"

"Before I'm through with you and your ilk," replied Bruce, "you'll learn better than to beat women." Bruce noticed the doctor looking at his watch. A slight smile crossed his face. "Three" his lips formed.

Omallin's face turned red with anger. He raved and he shouted at the taunting image. He tore a shock-rod from a Guard's hand, only to remember in time that it would fuse and hurt him.

Finally he quieted. "Stay there then, and watch. Watch what happens to this animal that insulted me. Barnes, give me that grid!"

A Polshin advanced with a broad flat disc of metal, perhaps a half-inch thick. A wire with a small plug trailed from it. Omallin grasped it, and shoved the plug into an accumulator pack he carried. He carried the heating grid over toward Lora. The doctor stepped in front of him.

"Please—you know the girl is sick. I think it would wait."

"Get out of the way, Manning. I don't care what you think. We need that information, and I want to teach that—"

"But—the girl's asleep," said Manning.

"She will wake quick enough."

"Oh, no, really, I'm afraid not. It's *delta-morphium*. Nothing can wake her within two days, you know. I thought it would hasten her recovery—"

Slowly Omallin's face went white with anger. His body quivered and wavelets dashed up his fat neck to break on the out-jutting reef of his chin. But there was nothing that would disturb Lora.

BRUCE turned to Philips. "Tom they're sending out the general call? Everyone knows the plan?"

"Yes, Bruce. They are beginning now, I think." He turned around and looked at the long row of electroscopes. Fifty men, seated before fifty sets of apparatus, were watching fifty different scenes. These fifty were all equipped with small projectors, capable of throwing voice, and, if necessary, a small scene. Quietly, low voices were speaking into the projector transmitters. "All of the Freedom Members will begin at once to carry out their parts under the General Plan—" Name after name was read out. All over the city the leaders were sending out their signals. The search of the city was barely well under way, it had not been called off by any means. But now—it ended abruptly. From eighty thousand apartments two hundred thousand people began to mill outward. In a moment, the Polshin guards were surrounded by masses of men, moving with such a deceptive air of slow determination, that the Polshins, who had never seen a planned, directed resistance, did not comprehend. Then they tried to use the tactics that had always served against the few half-hysterical attacks they had witnessed.

Their shock-rods glowing, they advanced on the nearest of the Plehbs, ordering them angrily back. Around each Polshin, six or eight Plehb men appeared, young, powerful Plehb men. Calmly they walked up to the Polshin guards. Crackling discharges of electricity sprang from the shock-rods—and rolled harmlessly off of the blue suits of the Plehbs. The Freedom Scientists had fulfilled their promise. Insulated suits had been distributed. Helpless, the Polshins were disarmed by men twice as strong as they were individually and numerically a hundred times as strong.

It was a wonderfully well-organized movement. Of the three thousand seven hundred and forty-two Polshin Guards, in that city that day, only three hundred and eleven were killed. Sometimes—hate was too strong. And every Plehb of the Freedom movement was equipped with death-dealing weapons now. Sometimes a Plehb would recognize in a captured Polshin the man who took away his mate, or his daughter. Took her into the horrible slavery, which every one of them had witnessed time and again on their telectroscopes. And from the least, lowest vertebrate, through all history, every male has fought hardest and most savagely for three things: life, his mate, and his offspring. And of those, perhaps his mate should come first. Never would so unified a movement have been possible without the telectroscope to show what happened to those poor creatures who were taken by the Polshins. It was a wonder so few were killed. Perhaps more would have been murdered had it not been that most of these Polshins were young men, some from foreign cities, and nearly all as yet unmarked by any Plehb as his own prey. And Bruce and his companions had worked hard, had taught and lectured, sought to prevent the venting of vengeance as cruel as anything the Polshins did. In some degree this had been effective, too. But most of all, many and many a Plehb had but a few minutes before seen that a Polshin need not necessarily mean an utterly cruel beast. That day Carl Manning saved a thousand lives.

BUT in half an hour, N'yak was in the hands of the Plehbs, utterly and completely. N'yak underground, that is. For above ground, the Polshins were prepared. With the first sign of the active rising, the Polshins had set up their defenses according to the rules their forefathers had lain down. Great ion guns were mounted before the mouth of every surface tube. The power controls had been cut—but the Plehb mechanics this time had destroyed the effect to be brought about by this move before it was made. Five material energy generators, each no larger than a man, had been set up, and were supplying all N'yak with abundant power. They had been set up and connected in, before the Polshins had cut the power controls.

Anxiously Bruce conferred with the men in other cities. In not every city had the rising occurred, only in those that felt certain of success. Eight of the cities of the Union were still under the rule of Polshins. Polshins patrolling in squads, with light ion guns under their arms.

But Bosn, Shkago, Felfya, all the cities which had been in the Union for any length of time, and possessed any number of proton-guns had revolted. The proton-guns were trained on the surface tubes by Plehbs, where they were not ready to drive out the Polshins unaided, and ion guns covered the tubes in cities where the Plehbs had the balance of power. In some places, both forces protected the tubes.

N'yak was ready for the next step. Overhead, the telectroscope showed atomic cruisers roaming ceaselessly, watching for any sign of attack. On the ground the surface crews in the gun-tanks, their mighty mounts crawling over the gardens and crushing ornamental bridges, prepared to aid the defense, to keep the rebel Plehbs below.

Bruce piloted the "Freedom I" as she sailed up through the hidden, unsuspected lock the Plehbs had built. Instantly, two huge atomic cruisers bore down on her. Their mighty ion-guns flaming destruction, the stone of the lock crackled in terrific heat, and the ground seemed to burst into flame. But the "Freedom" rode calmly nearer, the ion-flame splitting widely and washing off of her magnetic shield. A rain of the accumulator shells burst in intolerable flame on the outer surface of her momentum-wave driving field.

No material thing could reach the Freedom ships. One, two, finally four of the fighting ships of the N'yak Union had appeared. A dozen great atomic cruisers clustered and now their heavy radio-frequency beams began to bore in. Effortlessly, the slumberous giant of material energy smashed the ten million horsepower beams of the atomic cruisers to flaming static discharges.

Bruce moved. Slowly his fingers closed on the proton gun release. From the nose of his ship a blue-green tongue of energy, so stupendous as to be beyond measuring, drove out. Five hundred feet through the air the first discharge crashed its way, the two billion volt protons crushing the molecules of the air to hydrogen and sweeping them along. The electron discharge smashed out, then swiftly the alternations built up. Like a slow-licking solar prominence the unbelievable flame reached out—so slow seeming, yet so swift, the fleeing atomic cruiser vanished suddenly with but a slight alteration in the awful flame. Her magnetic shield was not built to resist two billion volt protons, nor the nearly two billion horsepower that drove them.

WITH a long-drawn roar of thunder, the column, the beam had built up for itself in the air, clapped shut, as Bruce cut off his proton tube. There was not so much as dust to fall back when it died. And now the flame licked out again, stretched, and another cruiser puffed into pure, blazing hydrogen gas. And Mother Earth sent up a great tongue of her own lightning in protest, a tongue of power, feeble and unreal in the frightful glare of the released giant of matter.

The atomic cruisers were fleeing toward the N'yak fortress now. After them the Freedom ships sent a flight of tiny bullets, bullets that glowed strangely as they tore along at speeds greater than meteors, leaving only the smashed ions of air to mark their tail. Driven from momentum-wave guns, they overtook the flying cruisers as readily as on old time rifle bullet overtook an airplane. One touched a cruiser. Instantly, without sound save the soft puff of a rising tongue of blue flame, the tail of the cruiser seemed to condense, collapse upon itself, then melt away. Disintegrator bullets had destroyed it—bullets that released electrostatic fields of such unimaginable intensity that the matter near them was torn to atoms. Not noisily and flashily, for noise and light are escaping energy, but so efficiently that they were quiet. Only the gaping hole in the tail of the cruiser told the story,

Slowly the five hundred-foot ship halted as the air resistance stopped her. Slowly her nose pointed downward, while a dim red glow rose to incandescence, telling of broken power-leads. She vanished altogether in five more sections as other bullets struck her.

And Bruce turned, and looked in vain for another enemy. Four Freedom ships rode unharmed in the air. The Polshin atomic cruisers were gone. No wreckage, no broken bodies remained. Only clear air.

And that day, at Mars Center, a scientist with a peculiarly fresh, youthful face, and deep age-old eyes, smiled as he told the president of the Martian State what he observed. "Earth will redeem your pledge to her soon, John. The seven centuries you mentioned have passed. Today, my instruments were upset badly. At first I thought a solar disturbance had done it. It came from the direction of Earth. It was an electric field—a field of an intensity we have never produced. Whatever caused it, anything within its influence must have been reduced to sub-atomic particles."

Bruce Lawry looked down at the fortress. The ten-foot tungsto-iridium walls loomed gray and stolid in the sunlight. A thousand feet in diameter, four hundred high, the fortress was scarred here and thereby the wars of the Old Days. But nothing had ever bitten deeply into her layers of magnetic and radio-frequency screening. No shell had pierced her. No heating ray reached through her screen. A ship, loaded with ultra-powerful explosive had driven at her in suicidal death. But the explosive had not reached her, only flying fragments of the ship.

THE N'Yak fortress was the most powerful in the world. Out of the range of its ion guns, Bruce was watching thoughtfully. Heavy rifles, hurling atomic explosives were firing angrily at him. A solid sheet of rippling flame roared around him, and despite its automatic balances, the "Freedom" wavered in their concussions. Bruce needed no telectroscope to see inside that metal walled fortress. Here was a steel-barred cell, a white bed, and a mass of dark, wavy hair, and a face with closed eyes, and warm, half-smiling lips. Smiling still in sleep over the joke played on Omallin, the joke in which she was the pawn. Behind those metal walls—

And Bruce could see also the dark-haired slim doctor with a blank look of stupidity on his face, and a deep, human twinkle in his dark eyes. Also behind those metal walls, Manning deserved Bruce's deepest consideration. But more still, by the side of Manning, Bruce seemed to see dozens, scores of Polshin figures, stalwart men—men for all that they were Polshins. Bruce had preached a doctrine and believed it. Despite what had happened, he could still believe it. Some of the Polshins in there were as truly victims of the system as was he, and any Plehb. Victims of a system that taught them utter inconsideration for Plehbs.

And that fort was not like the atomic cruisers. The fort was practically unlimited in its power, even though dependent on atomic rather than material energy. The fort could draw tremendous volumes of the cold, clear water from the broad river flowing near by, volumes great enough to carry away even the millions of horse power that would be lost through the inefficiency of the atomic engines. Then—there was no reason why that fort should not develop two billion or two hundred billion-horse power, at least for a short period. True, they used metallic conductors, unaided by the space-columns of the "Freedom" ships—but they used the ten-foot metal wall as a conductor for one polarity as Bruce knew. The other was led through silver pillars ten feet thick. Bruce felt sure he could have reduced it with a few hours struggle. Eventually, even those mighty metal conductors would have given way, for when atoms fight against energy conducted by space, the warp and woof of the universe, the outcome is foredoomed. His four cruisers could have arranged themselves broadside to the fort, allowing both stern and bow proton-tubes to come into action. Each ship turning the full power of those frightful ultra-atomic beams, driven by forces that made and broke suns, eight colossal tongues of energy, then the magnetic deflectors of the fort would have been loaded to the uttermost. And Bruce had still an untried weapon—the magnetic field with these raised also to their maximum, draining and weakening the field of the fort—

Bruce frowned. Earth would tremble to her core under the opposing stresses of those titanic engines. Her metal heart would strain upward and twist convulsively. N'yak, Felfya, Bosn, even Pizbur and Shkaga would be endangered by the upheavals resulting. N'yak, founded on a rock though she was, would slip slowly into the sea, for below, far below, the deepest level of the city, was the great geological fault line.

Yes—Bruce knew he could crack open that fort. Two things would happen. N'yak, and the territory for at least five hundred miles around it, would writhe and strain under the pulls of those struggling Titans. And—when finally the magnetic and electric defenses of the fort fell, they would inevitably fall abruptly, like an electric light bulb when the fuse blows out. And as quickly, the hundreds of billions of horsepower, struggling to break down those invisible walls of force, would wash in—and through. Beneath them, the ten-foot walls of practically infusible metal would vanish as a single magnificent tongue of burning hydrogen gas. The walls—and Lora. Lora, and every human thing within it.

SLOWLY Bruce looked at the men quietly waiting for his word. Without speaking, he tuned in the stage at Freedom Hall. Philips, Powr, a half-hundred others were looking at him, watching him.

"I can break open the fort in either a thousandth part of a billionth of a second—or within six hours. In either case, no single thing within that fort will continue to exist for even the briefest part of a second after the walls fall. And—N'yak will slide into the sea, and Mother Earth will strain and heave with the forces I must use. But—I could do it. What are we to do?"

"We cannot say," replied Powrs. "You are in complete command of all fighting. Bosn has reached the same position. Shkaga and Felfya. They are waiting for your lead."

"I will come there," decided Bruce.

Three ships remained circling the fort. Steadily the fort was sending out streams of every form of destruction they knew. Effortlessly the matter-giant brushed them aside. A tractor beam designed in the old days to pull down a full-fledged atomic battleship reached out, and tugged at one of the Freedom ships till the rocks of N'yak ground protestingly on each other. Effortlessly the material energies neutralized the pull with the greater power of the momentum waves.

Bruce returned slowly to Freedom Hall. They had won—and not won. It was stalemate now. What solution could they reach? The plan Lora had mentioned? Somehow that did not cover the conditions. It had seemed so simple and right to call down two ships from Felfya, to from Bosn and two from Shkaga, and combine to destroy the fort in that thousand billionth part of a second Bruce had mentioned. Now—new understanding, new contacts had changed the conditions.

Slowly Bruce stepped down from the hundred and fifty-foot ship as it landed in its berth.

CHAPTER ELEVEN

"I SUPPOSE," Omallin's image on the Freedom Hall stage was saying irritably, "those animals are observing us. Have we no privacy whatever left?"

Bruce could not resist the temptation. His image appeared on Omallin's right hand. But now he reduced his image to a foot-high figure. "No, Omallin. You have nothing any more. Neither privacy, nor power."

Omallin started violently, and pulled his hand away hastily. Then he swatted heavily at the foot-high image—and his hand passed through it unhindered. "Furthermore," Bruce continued, "we can crack that fort of yours like a rotten egg any time we want to."

"Hah," Omallin snorted angrily. "I didn't notice that you did it. A fort is a very different thing from a light atomic cruiser."

"Our Freedom ships are also very different. Your stupidity is too great for me to convince you short of actually destroying it. And then, of course, you would no longer exist. I may truly say that in all probability you will die unconvinced."

"Animal! For centuries we have proven our superiority, and when, for five minutes, you gain some slight advantage, you presume to claim the control."

Bruce shook his head slowly. "Animals—human beings. You are an animal also, Omallin. A swine I think. We are not only five minutes ahead of you. We are five thousand years ahead. We have all the civilization Earth ever had at our disposal, and with this very machine I have seen the face of the men living on the planets, from Mercury to Jupiter's moons.

"We have all you ever had, all we ourselves have developed—and all the things that the Planets have developed through the seven long centuries, while Earth slipped back and back to the vicious feudal system that produced you. Do you know that your Polshin President Mukarty in Washun is also in the great metal fortress there—surrounded by circling ships just like those over your heads? Your Polshin power has fallen. In some places advance is slower, since our organization is so new. Therefore we are waiting yet a little."

"The planets! The planets! Impossible," roared a Polshin councilor. "I have read the science of the Old Days and I know that no possible telescope could show such scenes."

Bruce laughed gently. "The latest record you have is surely seven centuries old. Look—and decide. This is Mars Center." In the place of Bruce's image, on the table in the N'yak fortress appeared a ten-inch globe of Mars, a globe that revolved with a majestic slowness that lent even this tiny image a mighty grandeur. The globe expanded till it was five feet through, then slowly the edges faded, till only one city, Mars Center, with its looming, stately towers, showed.

Then this vanished, and Jupiter with his nine moons, great and small, appeared, grew, and the great, sprawling city, Jove, centered on the table.

And Bruce reappeared. "Seven centuries the Planets have advanced—and we have done a bit ourselves.

"I am troubling to speak to you only because certain of the Polshins within your walls are fit to live. We can of course destroy that fort—but we would destroy some worthwhile lives. Even a few of our own.

"If you will lower your magnetic shields, we can promise life to some of you. And all of your people will be tried justly before a court of the men from the Planets. Do you know the Pledge of the Planets? Did your ancestors take down the words of John Montgommery that day when Interplanetary left Earth? They have waited, and they will help Earth now. Take down your walls, and accept trial. Otherwise—"

"Otherwise?" snorted Omallin. "Your bluff will fail. In all the wars of Earth, wars that would make your puny rebellion laughable, this fort was never so much as endangered.

"And—otherwise you will have to kill nearly three hundred of your own animal species. Including this Lora, who seems to be one of your leaders.

"I have a proposition in return," Omallin's fat lips smiled. "We can exist here forever, as you know. We like the gardens, however, so I will make this proposition. We will begin at once, and for nearly a whole year we can keep on, killing one of your animals each day—and all day long. The third one can be this Lora, for she will awake then. If you gain wisdom, you can turn over to us one of your Ships, your leaders, and these seeing machines. In return we will consider giving you certain privileges."

FROM beyond Bruce in the Freedom Hall came a mighty, angry roar of sound. It echoed through the transmitter, and into the metal-walled room where Omallin sat. A Plehb jumped up beside Bruce, and furiously he denounced the Polshins. "For every Plehb you harm—ten of the Polshins we have captured shall die as they die!"

Omallin shrugged. "It is not I," he replied. "That is the difference between such animals as you and a Polshin."

"Your stupidity is too great," sighed Bruce, returning to his position as the furious man was drawn away. "I was afraid you would believe nothing. However, I will give you two days to consider it. Also, we will communicate with others of the people within your fort."

"The first Plehb shall begin to die now," roared Omallin, rising to his feet, and shaking his fat fist at Bruce's figure, "and she shall pay for those repeated insults."

Bruce cut off the switch slowly, his face gray. He turned to the Freedom audience, and spoke slowly. "There seems to be nothing we can do. There is only one hope and a faint one. But I will try it. I have been studying at the University on Mars Central these past months—perhaps I have gained a new viewpoint that may help. Otherwise—there is nothing I can do. Since that is so—perhaps—it would be better—if we did not watch Omallin for a while."

Bruce left the platform, and hurried away to his laboratory. His fellow scientists were arriving rapidly now, returning to their work. Bruce called them to him, and rapidly gave to each of them an experiment to perform—all directed toward one end. And he himself worked at the one, determining, key experiment.

Each faint sound in the laboratory, each hum of apparatus and sound of low voices seemed to ring shrill in his ears.

Shrill—shrill as a tortured woman's scream heard through echoing corridors.

Bruce shook his head, and concentrated on the delicate task before him. Presently lathes began to turn, and the cry of the cut metal brought back the shrill ringing. Impatiently Bruce tossed his head, then bent lower, closer to his work.

Hours passed swiftly. Reports came in from outside, reports of progress in Bosn and Shkaga, in cities from San Friso to Myami. Everywhere Polshins were bottled up in fortresses, cut off from communication with the rest of the world by the washing, roaring static that the material energy engines were setting up now. No radio waves could penetrate it, and frightened Polshins conferred and trembled. But landlines, deep buried and protected, some secret and hidden, maintained communication between cities on the continent. All were waiting for the N'yak decision. Some had decided to try similar tactics. Bruce thought of that with an infinite pain. With freedom so near for those victims—this!

AND reports were coming from the scientists of the Freedom laboratories. In other cities, Freedom men were working, though here in N'yak, the best were gathered under Bruce. Working, seeking to do what they had never been able hitherto to accomplish.

The first day passed. And now the second dawned, and ceaselessly Bruce worked on. He would not sleep. Around him other men drove themselves on. But one by one they were forced to drop out as unsteady hands, weighted by fatigue, jarred delicate experiments into oblivion.

Bruce would not stop. But Dr. Grant finally stopped him with a bit of drug in the food Bruce allowed himself. For five hours Bruce would sleep, sleeping so intensively he would wake refreshed, as from twelve hours of sleep. His assistant

Director carried on the work, glimpsing vaguely the trend Bruce had established.

It was late in the second day when Bruce woke, furiously angry at first. Then he realized Dr. Grant's wisdom, and slipped back into his place.

First the reports of outside affairs came in. Half the Polshins in the N'yak fortress were nearly ready to believe the Plehbs could do as they claimed. The rest were utterly unconvinced. There would be no yielding on their part. Plehbs were animals.

A large Polshin audience had dropped in from time to time to witness Omallin's—resistance. Manning had risked his life for the Plehbs, and one hundred and three Plehbs slept now under delta-morphium for the full three days it allowed. But Manning was in a cell himself, awaiting action on Omallin's part.

A second victim was the object of Omallin's resistance now: he was adhering faithfully to his program. His first victim had died for twelve and a half hours.

Hurriedly Bruce turned to the Laboratory reports. He thought of Lora, not of the one assistant he needed most now, but of Lora, faintly stirring to wakefulness now, as the drug in her veins was gradually absorbed.

The laboratory reports were good—but somehow something seemed lacking. Rapidly his mind ran over every possible item that could help. It was a clearer, refreshed mind.

And then, in the way of man's mind, it functioned. A dog learns a trick slowly, by elimination of those moves, which produce no results. A man does not do the thing at all—or suddenly knows the whole secret, and the direct way to its accomplishment. Bruce saw.

With a sudden shout that stopped work over all the Laboratory he sprang to his feet. "Buck—Hal—Will—and

Brady, Come here." In syllables so swift his hearers could scarcely follow, he told them what he wanted. Instantly he turned to his task. The problem that had baffled them seemed solved!

In two hours, the first of the apparatus began to arrive, the new devices. Instantly Bruce and his assistants began setting it up, attaching it to the great telectroscope in Freedom Hall. In three hours, half the work was done, in four, it was completed. New apparatus, untried in connection, was ready. The transfer of *all* the electron waves was to be attempted! The transfer of not merely one ten-thousandth part of the whole—but *all* of it.

"I don't want to try it on a human—even yet—"

"Yes, you do, Bruce. There is one human—" interrupted Powers. "And we may hope by this time—that it fails in her case."

SLOWLY Bruce's color drained from his cheeks. With a steady hand he adjusted the great machine, focused it, and turned it on. A room appeared in the N'yak fortress. A bare metal room, with a half-dozen scarlet figures. Five of them were Polshins, scarlet because of their clothing. The sixth—

Bruce worked with all the rapidity he could muster. One of the Polshins was wrapping electric resistance wire around the sixth figure, a bound, softly moaning figure. Cautiously Bruce advanced a control, and a light, hazy outline surrounded the sixth figure on the Freedom Hall stage. Under Bruce's manipulation the haze condensed, and only the additional solidification told of the added apparatus's work. Abruptly Bruce drove home a plunger switch. A mighty humming roar echoed through the great auditorium, the straining pull of the matter-giant, as the entire structure of the Universe was altered by one small fraction.

Then it died, died as abruptly as it had come. On the stage the sixth form crumpled slowly to the floor. The five others started back in amazement and terror—then rushed forward to pass their hands through the spot where the material, physical body now lay. Bruce had set up a new electron-wave pattern, and instantaneously the electrons, the protons, then atoms that had made up that girl's body, simply *weren't* where they had been, but in a new position—on Freedom Hall stage.

Dr. Grant was kneeling over the blood stained figure. She was moaning no longer. Bruce joined him, tense and white. Slowly, the doctor turned his face up to Bruce. "I'm sorry Bruce—life is too marvelously delicate a balance for the titanic forces you need to hurl matter out of existence, and back into existence elsewhere. It was not her condition. The vitameter shows that every individual cell is dead, even the lowest types, the hair cells and finger nail cells—though that may be because of what they did to her.

"I think that you have set yourself an impossible task, Bruce. How much power did you use in doing this?"

"Three and one-half hundred billion horsepower hours. I killed her."

"She would thank you Bruce, you know that. But don't you see that such a titanic power—more than even this whole city uses in a year—is too much for life to be associated with?"

"When will Lora wake, Grant?" asked Bruce softly.

Grant looked at his wristwatch. "She should wake about now or soon, Bruce."

"I will bring her—when she wakes." Slowly Bruce sat down. He looked at the great machine with dull eyes. Utter quiet reigned in Freedom Hall. A pair of soft-shod hospital attendants came, and covered the body on the stage. Softly they carried it away.

Every eye seemed turned on them as they walked unhindered through the immaterial images that were dashing madly about on the stage, noiseless, unreal.

Then Bruce laughed, softly and with such genuine mirth that Dr. Grant turned to him with a face suddenly whiter and more drawn than before. Bruce looked up at him with a smiling, teasing face. There was nothing insane in that face.

"No, I'm all right Grant. Everything's all right. You see, just for a moment I wasn't thinking, because everything was so concentrated on that hope of bringing Lora out of the fortress that way. But just think—look."

Again Bruce was at the controls. In an instant the scene had shifted, it was Lora's cell now, the girl stirring slowly to consciousness on her bed. Bruce projected himself, and his image bent over by the side of Lora's bed.

"Lora," he said, "Lora dear—it's Bruce." Slowly the lids raised, the long lashes curved upward.

"Bruce—the joke worked, didn't it?"

She paused, suddenly fuller consciousness returned, and the laughing glint in her eyes changed. They were suddenly very intent and thoughtful. "Bruce, what did you call me?"

"I called you Lora—Lora, dear. Do you mind?"

"Oh—," sudden animation carne to her. She sat up abruptly, clutching the blanket to her. "Then—then I'm not—your laboratory assistant."

Bruce smiled. "I suppose you are—but that's not all."

With that point settled, other things could reach Lora's consciousness. She saw for the first time the steel bars that had been there when she fell into the long sleep. "Bruce—where am I? In the same place?" There was fright in her voice now. "I've been here two days? You couldn't get in?"

"Not till five minutes ago, Lora. I have now, though. I can transport matter entire by the process, transport it as far as I can project an image of normal size."

"Then you can get me out?"

A cloud came over his face. "No, Lora, I have tried it, and it won't transport life. Dr. Grant says the forces involved are too mighty for life to endure. I tried once, but—but the experiment failed. It's all right though, because you see, dear, no substance in all the Universe can endure these forces. See, your bars." Bruce's image vanished from the cell, but there was a sudden enormous tension, a tension that seemed to draw at her very soul. Quietly, without a sound, the great steel door dissolved away—quietly as the noiseless ships of the Freedom Union—the quietness of the Matter Giant at work.

Bruce reappeared. "I have other work to do with this now. Omallin wouldn't surrender. I couldn't break down his magnetic defenses without rocking Earth to her heart. So now I must leave you for a brief while, dear, while I finish the work. I will bring you a white robe of the Freedom Union, and a telectroscope, and the twin tubes before I go though."

He melted away again, and where he had been, a white robe, a small telectroscope, and the twin pistols of the Freedom Union came gently into existence. Laughing in her heart, Lora rose, and went to them.

Fat Omallin was quivering and ordering and shrieking threats and vengeance. Two score Polshins, most of them young Polshin Guardsmen, were watching the performance with growing signs of disgust. The more Omallin realized their feelings, the more their barbs penetrated his thick intellectual hide, the more he disintegrated. His eyes were wide and frightened in their folds.

Gradually a cold silence fell about him, and his voice died slowly into silence too. Steady, hard-eyed gazes were bent on him. These young men saw in him for the first time the weakness and degeneracy that he represented.

A low voice spoke, from the air, "Disgusting performance, Omallin. It won't do you any good anyway. I told you I could crack that nutshell of yours anytime I wanted to. Omallin, will you come down to the power-room with me?"

OMALLIN shrieked as a *solid* something pushed him gently. Fast as his fat legs could carry him he ran for his own private room. A solid something turned him aside at the doorway, pushed him, forced him toward the power room. Whimpering, his face glazed with a cold sweat, he was forced along. There was solidity in the image now, not absolute solidity, but enough to force him.

Behind him trailed some forty-five Polshin Guardsmen. Down the corridor they went, then down an elevator that mysteriously took on volition of its own, down to the depths beneath the ground level, into the lowest level of the N'yak Fortress. There was a great, smooth, humming roar here. Rivers of cold water, nearly five million gallons a minute, were rushing through the huge pumps. The great atomic generators hummed and chuckled softly to themselves, the half-dozen Polshin Wartechs, who ran them, seeming tiny among their gray bulks. Long silver columns led across the vast cavern to apparatus on the same Titan's scale.

"I didn't want to do it," said the voice calmly," because we would have wracked old Mother Earth in the doing. So I'll do it this way. I'll take Burner I of bank, A first, I think—"

Bruce wasn't gentle this time, and besides, instead of merely bringing it back to the N'yak Hall, he was throwing it away, out in space a hundred thousand miles from Earth. The soul-wrenching tension built up, and suddenly there was a terrible, ear-tearing scream, the scream as of a living animal in pain, almost—

The outlines of the first of the big generators faded away, in its deep interior they could see the burning fires. Then the fires blossomed in a sudden explosion of heat and light for a billionth of a second, a vast flower of blue-violet flame.

Then there was nothing. Only the thunderous roar of the air rushing in to fill a sudden vacuum.

There were ten of those thunderous roars. Ten times the whole vast N'yak Fortress shuddered to them and in her cell fifteen floors above, Lora smiled as she heard them. Bruce was not being gentle, as he tore the living heart out of the N'yak Fortress.

"I think you'd better start back," said Bruce. "I'm going to take two of the pump battery now." Omallin realized suddenly that the solid thing had released him. His legs pumped desperately up the ramp to the elevator. It would still work, as the lights still worked, for the accumulators remained, intact and charged. Behind him he heard again two roaring blasts—and a new sound. The sound of thundering, rushing water. Water draining in the opened forty-foot ducts from the Hudson and the Atlantic. Presently, as the elevator, loaded to capacity, began its slow rise, Omallin heard the crackle and spit of shorted electrical circuits.

His face was pasty when he stepped from the elevator at his own level. The Polshin Guardsmen were still with him.

And—the voice was still with him. It was hard now. Hard and grim and stern. "Omallin, I wanted you to see that, and to know your power was definitely crushed. You are so savagely, horribly monstrous, so utterly inhuman and beyond human consideration, so far-gone in the depths of the degeneracy, the worlds *need* you. You should be preserved for all time, so that men may know what they can fall to."

Omallin didn't get the sense of what Bruce said. He only heard "the worlds need you" and "preserved for all time," and a look of cunning hope spread over his face. The eyes slitted once more—perhaps a bargain remained to him—life and Plehb girls too, perhaps—

His face remained that way. Bruce saw it, and realized that never again could he hope for so perfect an expression. A terrible tension built up in the room, a tension that leapt and crackled in static discharges like miniature lightning, roaring and snapping, driving back the Polshin Guardsmen from about Omallin. And Omallin remained rigid, the same expression fixed on his face. But slowly, something was happening to him as the Matter Giant tore and strained and pushed at the atoms that made him. He was shrinking, and his color was fading. Slowly he shrank, and slowly the color faded, and a strange luster came, a dull silvery luster—

Three minutes passed before the tension vanished, and the shrinking stopped. Then—Omallin stood on the floor. On his face was the same expression of leering, cunning lust, the same fat jowls and pouched eyes. But there was no color in the face, and it was a face gleaming with a dull, smooth metallic luster. And Omallin stood only some few inches tall, but he was really quite valuable, even in those days, for he was solid iridium, every atom of him, and he weighed two hundred and ninety pounds, just as he had before.

Forty-five Polshin Guardsmen, their faces as white as the metal face of the statuette that would endure for untold millenia unchanged, uncorroded, stormed down the wide hallway—anywhere away—

EPILOGUE

JOHN MONTGOMMERY'S age-old eyes, in their setting in his fresh, youthful face, were burning with a light of happiness. Bruce Lawry and Lora stood before him on the platform of Interplanetary Hall at Mars Center. Beside them stood a telectroscope, and on its stage was an image of Freedom Hall in N'yak, one hundred and thirty-seven million, five hundred thousand miles away.

"You, Bruce Lawry, can have no conception of my feelings in greeting you officially here. You have not lived through my more than seven hundred years, you have not waited while thirty generations of men came and went about you, waited through decades and through centuries hoping always to hear from the planet it has been your duty to isolate from all contact with her sister worlds, waited and wondered what things were going on.

"Six months ago our scientists first announced that they had detected across all the gulf of space the tremendous force-fields you were using, and for the first time the centuries of waiting seemed insupportable.

"In the Pledge of the Planets, seven centuries ago I promised that the planets would help Earth in settling her problems. I said you must come with a new ship, bringing a new invention. You have come bringing such gifts as we have never imagined possible. You have shown us exact images of planets circling a star three hundred and fifty-seven light-years distant. You have shown us matter at the heart of the sun, and matter in the very nebulae.

"And unaided, Earth has all but settled her own problems.

"It is Earth who should welcome us back into the intercourse of Planets," Montgommery paused. Then from the table he took a small metal key. For long seconds he looked at it, then slowly raised his face to Bruce Lawry.

"Seven centuries ago I watched while this key was cut. I wondered then how long it would be in our vaults.

"Today I brought it out. You cannot know my happiness in giving to you this key to the Sealed Chamber. Never again will I have to pass that closed door with the memories and thoughts I have endured."

THE END

If you've enjoyed this book, you will not want to miss these terrific titles…

ARMCHAIR SCI-FI & HORROR DOUBLE NOVELS, $12.95 each

D-101 **THE CONQUEST OF THE PLANETS** by John W. Campbell
THE MAN WHO ANNEXED THE MOON by Bob Olsen

D-102 **WEAPON FROM THE STARS** by Rog Phillips
THE EARTH WAR by Mack Reynolds

D-103 **THE ALIEN INTELLIGENCE** by Jack Williamson
INTO THE FOURTH DIMENSION by Ray Cummings

D-104 **THE CRYSTAL PLANETOIDS** by Stanton A. Coblentz
SURVIVORS FROM 9,000 B. C. by Robert Moore Williams

D-105 **THE TIME PROJECTOR** by David H. Keller, M.D. and David Lasser
STRANGE COMPULSION by Philip Jose Farmer

D-106 **WHOM THE GODS WOULD SLAY** by Paul W. Fairman
MEN IN THE WALLS by William Tenn

D-107 **LOCKED WORLDS** by Edmond Hamilton
THE LAND THAT TIME FORGOT by Edgar Rice Burroughs

D-108 **STAY OUT OF SPACE** by Dwight V. Swain
REBELS OF THE RED PLANET by Charles L. Fontenay

D-109 **THE METAMORPHS** by S. J. Byrne
MICROCOSMIC BUCCANEERS by Harl Vincent

D-110 **YOU CAN'T ESCAPE FROM MARS** by E. K. Jarvis
THE MAN WITH FIVE LIVES by David V. Reed

ARMCHAIR SCIENCE FICTION CLASSICS, $12.95 each

C-34 **30 DAY WONDER**
by Richard Wilson

C-35 **G.O.G. 666**
by John Taine

C-36 **RALPH 124C 41+**
by Hugo Gernsback

ARMCHAIR SCI-FI & HORROR GEMS SERIES, $12.95 each

G-11 **SCIENCE FICTION GEMS, Vol. Six**
Edmond Hamilton and others

G-12 **HORROR GEMS, Vol. Six**
H. P. Lovecraft and others

HOW WOULD YOU LIKE TO GO TO THE MOON?

It was only natural that Professor Banning should want to expand his knowledge of outer space and the solar system. So the moon, being of particular interest to him, became his next "project." He enlisted two assistants: one was the most famous pilot of the time, and the second was a man so smart he could build just about anything the professor could dream up. Together they built a rocket ship designed to take them deep into space.

This is the story of three brave men as they set out on the longest journey ever undertaken by man—a trip to the moon and back. Join golden age sci-fi author Bob Olsen as he spins a truly ingenious tale of lunar adventure and daring travel across the infinite vacuum of outer space, first published in Amazing Stories *way back in 1931.*

ABOUT BOB OLSEN...

Bob Olsen was born in Rhode Island on April 12, 1884. He was an American science fiction writer, whose real name was Alfred Johannes Olsen. Author of several poems, and short stories, he often wrote humorous science fiction in *Amazing Stories*, from 1927 to 1936. Then he wrote for other sci-fi publications until 1957. He was one of the first writers to use the phrase "space marine." The earliest known use of the term "space marine" was in his short story "Captain Brink of the Space Marines", a light-hearted work whose title is a play on the song "Captain Jinks of the Horse Marines", and in which the protagonists were marines of the "Earth Republic Space Navy" on mission to rescue celebrity twins from aliens on Titan. Olsen published a novella sequel four years later, "The Space Marines and the Slavers", featuring the same characters using a spaceship with active camouflage to free hostages from Martian space pirates on Ganymede.

Bob Olsen passed away in Ventura County, California on May 20th, 1956.

THE MAN WHO ANNEXED THE MOON

By
BOB OLSEN

ARMCHAIR FICTION
PO Box 4369, Medford, Oregon 97504

*For more information about Armchair Books and products, visit our
website at…*

www.armchairfiction.com

Or email us at…

armchairfiction@yahoo.com

CHAPTER ONE
Banning's Astounding Proposal

"BOYS! How would you like to accompany me on a voyage of exploration to the moon?" The speaker was Professor Archimedes Banning, and the "boys" to whom he addressed this nonchalant but startling proposal were Colonel Charles Berglin and myself.

Judging from the expression on his face, Berglin was surprised. Not I, however, I had known the alert, though elderly scholar too long and too well to be astonished at anything he said or did.

Professor Banning was a scientific Alexander the Great. No matter how amazing or how stupendous were the feats he accomplished, he was always looking for new worlds to conquer.

To savants throughout the world, Professor Banning was known as *the* authority on the fourth dimension and non-Euclidian geometry.

The general public, however, knew him best as the inventor of the *Spirit of Youth*—the first successful space flyer.

You will doubtless recall the intense interest and excitement, which was engendered throughout the world several years ago when the *Spirit of Youth* made its epochal flight around the moon. On that occasion the space flyer, after circumnavigating the moon, had returned to the Earth without stopping.

Despite the fact that no landing was made on our satellite, this unprecedented feat demonstrated beyond question the feasibility of interplanetary travel.

The event was all the more notable because the *Spirit of Youth* was piloted by no less a personage than Colonel

Charles Berglin, the most famous aviator that had ever lived. Professor Banning acted in the capacity of interplanetary navigator.

It was somewhat of an accident that made it possible for me—an obscure nonentity—to accompany this famous pair on their memorable journey.

Shortly after he had resigned from his position as Professor of Mathematics at Green University in my native state of Rhode Island, Professor Banning had employed me as a sort of mechanical obstetrician for the inventions which were constantly being born in his fecund mind.

I was selected partly because I was a graduate mechanical engineer, but principally on account of the special work I had done in the more advanced and complex branches of mathematics.

Thanks to what Professor Banning was kind enough to call a rare combination of mechanical skill and the ability to grasp the complicated principles and formulas of pure mathematics, I was lucky enough to get this desirable job.

Professor Banning insisted on placing me under a contract. By its terms I received a very satisfactory salary whether or not there was any work for me to do. But the pecuniary compensation was the least of the benefits I derived from this connection. My close association with the learned scholar, besides being a source of pleasure, was a liberal education in itself.

When Professor Banning had broached to Berglin and me his intention of conducting a second expedition, this time landing on the moon and exploring its surface, Berglin's answer was characteristically brief and courageous: "O.K., with me, chief. If you feel sure it can be done and you want my help, you can count on me."

To me was left my customary role of critic and objector.

"Do you really think it is possible to alight on the moon?" I questioned. "How are you going to land without crashing when there's no atmosphere to support the airfoils?"

"That's easy," was the Professor's comeback. "We'll use the rocket tubes at the front and bottom of the flyer as brakes. There's absolutely no reason—either theoretical or practical—why we shouldn't light as softly as a feather."

Perhaps I should explain, for the benefit of those who may not have given close attention to the newspaper accounts of its maiden voyage, that the *Spirit of Youth* combined the principle of an airplane with the addition of rocket tubes, which were used for navigating the airless space between the Earth and the moon.

MY second question was: "How about taking off from the moon on the return trip?"

"Again we'll use the rockets. You probably know that on the moon everything is much lighter than on Earth; consequently the hop-off from the moon ought to be the easiest part of the entire trip."

"But the space surrounding the moon is a perfect vacuum, isn't it?"

"Hardly a perfect vacuum, I'd say. That the moon has no atmosphere even comparable to the more rarefied air at the tops of the Earth's highest mountains has been proved beyond the shadow of a doubt, but most authorities believe that the moon has a very slight amount of gaseous envelope. The nearest approach to a vacuum obtainable under the bell jar of a mechanical air pump would probably come pretty close to duplicating the atmosphere of the moon."

"If that's the case, how could we get the door of our flyer open without losing all the air from inside the cabin?"

"I'm surprised at you—supposedly a mechanical expert—asking a question as stupid as that. Haven't you ever heard of air locks? Don't you know it is a simple matter to devise a small chamber with one airtight door communicating with the cabin and the other with the space outside? Do I need to go any further?"

"No," was my shamefaced reply. "I'll have to admit that was a dumb question, but here's one that I hope you won't think quite so stupid: If people have nosebleeds, hemorrhages and become violently ill, just from being in the rarefied atmosphere of high altitudes on Earth, what would happen to us if our bodies were surrounded by an almost perfect vacuum? Wouldn't we just blow up and burst—just like the deep sea fishes do when they are suddenly drawn from the high pressures of the ocean's depths to the relatively low pressure of the Earth's atmosphere?"

"That's much better, my boy. I'm glad to see you have some intelligence left. It is quite possible that something like that would happen if we attempted to step forth on the moon without adequate protection. But I've already designed a species of armor or vacuum suit that will easily take care of this contingency. I'll tell you all about it later. Are there any other objections?"

The only one I could think of was: "A contraption strong enough to protect a man against the terrific forces to which he would be subjected would have to be pretty heavy, wouldn't it?"

"Not necessarily, as I shall demonstrate to you shortly. My device ought not to weigh more than two hundred pounds. But suppose it weighs half a ton, what of it?"

"How in the world could anyone but a professional strong man manipulate a weighty and cumbersome contrivance like that without help?"

"If we tried to use such a suit on Earth it would indeed be difficult. But don't forget that everything weighs less on the moon. This is due to the fact that weight varies directly with the mass of the attracting body. The moon has only about one-thirteenth as much volume as the Earth. On the other hand, the moon is made of lighter material. Using water as the standard, the density of the Earth is five point five three and that of the moon only three point three six. From this you can easily figure out that the force of gravitation on the moon is only about one-sixth as great as on the Earth.

"This means that if you, when dressed in full armor, weighed one thousand pounds on the Earth, you would find it as easy to move around on the moon as if the whole outfit, including yourself, weighed only one hundred, and eighty pounds.

"You weigh a hundred and fifty pounds, don't you?"

"A hundred and forty-eight."

"It wouldn't be much of a job for you to carry a load of thirty-two pounds, would it?"

"Hardly."

"But you won't even have to do that, I'm confident that we can make a suit that will do the work and will weigh less than two hundred pounds. That will make you actually weigh about sixty pounds when you start your promenades on the moon. You'll be more likely to be bothered because you'll be too light rather than too heavy, or I miss my prognostication.

"And now have I answered all your questions satis-factorily?"

"Yes, Professor. I'm satisfied."

"If that's the case there seems to be no reason on Earth—or on the moon either—why such an expedition is not entirely feasible.

"And think of the glory! What we have accomplished so far is nothing compared with the honor of being the first men to set foot on the moon!"

The professor's enthusiasm was so contagious that there was no escaping the infection. The inevitable happened, of course. Both Berglin and I pledged our support to Professor Banning's enterprise and we immediately started work carrying out the details of his well thought-out plans.

CHAPTER TWO
The Banning Space Flyer

SINCE the *Spirit of Youth* had demonstrated its efficiency as a space flyer by completing the round trip between the Earth and the moon, I naturally took it for granted that our second voyage would be made in the same conveyance.

But Professor Banning had other plans.

"The *Spirit of Youth* is a fine machine," he told me one day. "It was built for a certain purpose and it served that purpose well. But the present task is somewhat different. Our first trip through interplanetary space taught us several lessons and we'd be foolish if we didn't profit by them, I therefore propose to build a brand new space flyer, specifically designed for transportation between the Earth and the moon."

Constructing a large machine of original and revolutionary design naturally required a lot of time and cost a lot of money, but neither of these items seemed to bother Professor Banning. Thanks to the royalties which for many years had accrued from the sale of his mathematics text books, augmented by the income from a number of sage investments, Professor Banning was independently wealthy.

For building those portions of the ship, which were of conventional pattern, such as the fuselage and landing gear, we used the staff of the Bryan Aircraft Corporation at San Diego, which had been placed at our disposal.

Most of my time was spent in working out the mechanical details of the unique features of the flyer.

While built somewhat on the plan of a large airplane of the enclosed cabin type, our space flyer embodied several revolutionary and peculiar features. One of these was the unusually small proportions of the airfoils, which were less than one-third the ordinary size. Theoretically, we could have dispensed with wings entirely, since the rocket principle of propulsion did not require them. The reason why Professor Banning included small wings as part of his design was that by their aid our craft could be handled more easily and at a much smaller consumption of fuel during the passage through the Earth's atmospheric envelope.

The most radical departure from standard airplane design was the elimination of the propeller and of the internal combustion motor. In their place were substituted a system of rocket tubes and combustion chambers which were so simple and so light that they made possible a substantial increase in the pay load.

To the selection of a suitable fuel Professor Banning devoted a great deal of study and research. After he had made hundreds of unsatisfactory tests with various types of gases, volatile liquids and other substances, the problem was solved for him in an utterly unexpected way.

Through a small item in a local newspaper he learned that Captain Frank Sims, one of the world's greatest authorities on high explosives, was living in Los Angeles. Possibly you will remember Captain Sims as the man who originated BRT, the explosive used in the depth bomb which played much havoc among German submarines during the World War.

Professor Banning visited Captain Sims in the hope of getting some suggestions regarding fuel for his space flyer.

He learned that Captain Sims had recently perfected a new explosive which was over four times as powerful as TNT, and which could be handled even carelessly with absolute safety. It was in the form of a fine powder, and was known as radatomite.   At the time of Professor Banning's call, arrangements had just been completed for the manufacture of radatomite on a large scale.

When he learned of our plans to explore the moon, Captain Sims not only agreed to turn over to us the first output of his factory at cost price, but also collaborated with Professor Banning in inventing an ingenious and remarkably efficient device for exploding the powder and controlling the discharge through the rocket nozzles with safety and certainty.

SINCE this is not a treatise on mechanics, I shall omit a detailed description of the combustion chambers, which Professor Banning and Captain Sims invented for regulating the discharges of radatomite through the rocket tubes. Though ingenious beyond comparison, this device was beautifully simple, and for that reason it functioned perfectly, with practically no likelihood of ever getting out of order.

According to the plans of our space flyer most of the propulsive force was to be directed through four rocket tubes, which terminated at the tail of the ship, all of them pointing dead astern. By means of an ordinary hand throttle, the stream of burning Radatomite could be controlled with marvelous exactitude, ranging from a faint fizz like the discharge of a tiny toy rocket to a continuous blast of expanding gases more powerful than the mightiest of tornadoes.

At the nose of the flyer were four more rocket tubes pointing straight ahead. A separate throttle regulated the radatomite discharges through these tubes, which served the purpose of brakes for use when it was desired to decrease or completely neutralize the forward speed of the flyer. They could even be used for flying the machine in reverse.

For steering purposes two tubes were carried to the tip of the right wing and two to the left. One of each pair pointed forward and the other toward the rear.

In the place of the propeller was a vertical beam, the lower end of which just cleared the ground when the flyer was taxiing. At each end of this beam were two more rocket tubes, one pointed ahead and the other astern.

These eight steering tubes were operated by means of a standard type of airplane joystick. Pushing the stick to the right would produce currents of exploding radatomite through both the tubes pointing to the rear at the left tip of the wing and the one pointing forward at the right tip—thus turning the nose of the machine to the right. To steer in the opposite direction, it was only necessary to move the stick to the left.

The tubes at the extremities of the upright beam took the place of the elevator, steering the flyer upward or downward according to whether the joystick was moved backward or forward. When the stick was in a neutral position, no gas whatever flowed through the steering tubes. The strength of the currents produced by exploding radatomite shooting through these pipes was determined by the distance which the stick was moved away from the perpendicular position.

Thus far, with the possible exception of the apparatus for controlling the rate of discharge through the rocket tubes, there was nothing original or revolutionary about the design of our flyer. In its general get-up it was quite similar to other rocket planes, which had either been described or planned, or worked out in model form by scientists both in America and in Europe.

There was at least one feature of the Banning space flyer, however, which was absolutely original and unique, and that was the four-dimensional steering device.

Constructing the mechanical contrivance, which made it possible for the flyer actually to be steered into hyperspace, was the special job assigned to me.

Though I completed this astonishing task successfully, I was able to do it only because of the cooperation and close supervision, which I received, from Professor Banning.

I shall not attempt a detailed explanation of this complicated device since—to be perfectly frank—I'm not sure I understand it fully myself—in spite of the fact that I made every bit of it with my own hands.

Fortunately, I was present at a time when Professor Banning was explaining the four dimensional principle to Colonel Berglin, and the following transcript of this exposition is much clearer and more comprehensive than I could possibly make it.

CHAPTER THREE
Professor Banning Explains the Fourth Dimension

RESPONDING to a request from Colonel Berglin to explain the four dimensional steering mechanism to him, Professor Banning said: "When you fly an airplane you have three different lines of motion to consider: one you call forward or backward, another left or right, and the third up or down.

"On our space flyer, these three lines of direction are well represented by our three systems of rocket tubes. Motion forward and backward is produced by the tubes at the bow and the stern; motion to the right or left is controlled by the tubes at the tips of the wings, and motion up or down is regulated by the tubes at the extremities of our elevating beam.

"If you imagine lines drawn to indicate these directions, they would be three in number and could be made to point in such a way that anyone of them is exactly perpendicular to each of the other two.

"If we measure the extension of our flyer along each of these lines the figure we obtain will represent the three dimensions, length, width and height.

"Further than that the ordinary mind does not attempt to go. But to the trained mathematician it is easy to conceive of a *fourth* dimension, or line of direction, and to place this line in such a way that it is perpendicular to all of the lines representing the other three dimensions. Is that clear?"

"I think I get what you're driving at," Berglin answered. "But I don't see how it is possible to draw a line in such a way that it will be perpendicular to three other lines at the same point."

"That's because you've always been accustomed to thinking of things as having only three dimensions. I don't mean to imply that all the things with which we are familiar extend for any considerable distance in the fourth dimension, but I do know that every object in the universe has at least a small amount of four-dimensional extension.

"Perhaps I can clarify this point by making comparison with objects which are commonly regarded as being two-dimensional in character—a piece of tissue paper, for instance. We all know that even the thinnest of materials must have some thickness, yet this dimension may be so small in comparison with the other two that a person accustomed only to thin, flat objects could easily assume that the paper had only two dimensions, namely length and width.

"Now suppose this Flatlander should happen to take a large number of pieces of thin paper and pile them on top of each other. Can't you see how he could thus discover the existence of a third dimension even if he had previously had knowledge of only two dimensions?"

"Yes, I can see that plainly enough," Berglin rejoined.

"Well, that's all there is to understanding the fourth dimension. Just imagine a lot of three-dimensional objects grouped together in such a way that they extend in a direction that is neither east or west, north or south, nor up or down, but at the same time is at right angles to each of these directions, and you have a clear conception of the fourth dimension.

"When you want to construct a four dimensional counterpart of any particular geometrical figure, all you have to do is figure out how you would construct a corresponding three dimensional article from two dimensional units and your problem solves itself.

"For instance, if you want to build a cube you can do it by piling together a large number of squares of the same size cut out of paper until you have a pile as high as one edge of your original square. Likewise, if you wish to construct a four-dimensional cube—which, by the way, is called a tesseract—you can do it by combining three-dimensional cubes.

"Take another example. To make a cylinder out of two-dimensional units, all you have to do is combine a large number of pieces cut in the shape of a circle. Hence a four dimensional cylinder would be composed of the three dimensional counterparts of the circles, namely solid spheres.

"To steer our flyer into hyperspace by means of our rocket principle it is necessary to construct tubes having extension in the fourth dimension. If you were a Flatlander and wanted to make a pipe out of tinfoil, how would you do it?"

"That's easy," said Berglin. "I'd make a roll out of it."

I knew at once that this was not the answer the Professor was fishing for and I couldn't help smiling just a wee bit at the look of disapproval which Berglin's common-sense suggestion brought to Banning's face.

"That's wrong!" he shouted. "The minute you bend a roll of tinfoil you get completely out of your two dimensional environment. What I mean is, how could you build a pipe by combining a large number of articles, all of which must be absolutely flat and extremely thin?"

"Oh, I see what you mean now. They'd have to be in the form of rings or washers."

"Exactly! Now you're beginning to grasp the idea. Suppose for the sake of convenience we call your rings or washers hollow circles. Now what sort of units shall we require for building our four dimensional pipe?"

"Hollow spheres, I suppose."

"Precisely. And that's how we made our four dimensional rocket tubes. We combined a large number of hollow spheres in such a way as to make a continuous passageway, through which currents of gases resulting from the combustion of our fuel can be projected, either into or away from hyperspace.

"This sounds simple enough but in actual practice it requires a knowledge of certain principles of higher mathematics which cannot be comprehended except by a person who has spent years in studying them. The difficult thing is to know just how to group the hollow spheres together. You can readily understand that they cannot be placed one in front of the other, one beside the other or one on top of the other, since that would mean merely producing additional extension in either length, width or height. Instead, they have to be placed THROUGH each other and in such a way that the hollow spaces combine to make one continuous hole through which the gases can pass. Do you understand what I mean?"

"I guess I do, but when you talk about sticking together a lot of hollow balls in such a way that gas can pass through the hollow spaces, you're getting way ahead of me."

"That's very simple if you think of these balls as being open in the direction of the fourth dimension, just as a washer or ring is open in the third dimension.

"To a two-dimensional being it would be as impossible to put anything inside a ring as for us to do the same thing to a hollow ball. Yet one of us can easily pick up a small article from outside and drop it inside the ring. In the same way, by moving through the fourth dimension, you could pick up a pebble and place it inside a tennis ball without making any opening in the rubber. It is also possible to combine hollow spheres in such a way as to form a gas-tight tube."

"That's mighty interesting, even though I'm afraid I don't grasp it completely," Berglin responded. "Your explanation is entirely different from the conception of the fourth dimension I had before. Somehow or other I got the idea that the fourth dimension is time. I remember reading a book called "The Time Machine." It's about a contraption, which was supposed to be able to travel in the fourth dimension. With it a man could either go clear back into the days of ancient history or could travel ahead and see how the world is going to be thousands of years in the future."

To which the Professor replied, "Fantastic tales like that are not intended to be taken seriously. They make interesting yarns but couldn't possibly be true. I don't mean to deprecate the so-called scientific fiction stories as a class. Many of them, like 'Twenty Thousand Leagues Under the Sea,' which were originally written as the wildest and most impossible imaginative fiction have already been made real through modern inventions. But when you try to conceive of seeing events eons before they actually happen, common sense tells us that even the most marvelous of scientific discoveries could never make such a thing possible."

HERE I took the liberty of butting in on the dialogue. "Excuse me, Professor," I ventured. "But doesn't Einstein's theory of relativity regard time as a fourth dimension?"

"In one sense, perhaps, but that's a mere matter of terminology," he continued. "The essential idea behind the principle of relativity is that every object in the universe is moving. There's no such thing as absolute rest. And since objects move at different speeds, it is impossible to obtain an accurate measure of the distance between two objects unless we know the speed with which each of the objects, as well as the observer, is traveling.

"There's where the time element enters and it's sometimes referred to, rather loosely, as the fourth dimension. The term 'separation interval' is a much better word in my opinion, since that suggests both time and distance.

"I don't believe that even Einstein would presume to believe that time is a dimension like length, along which one can travel either forward or backward and at varying speeds.

"On the other hand, the geometrical fourth dimension which I have just explained to you has nothing to do with time. It is a real spacial extension, of exactly the same character as length, width and thickness.

"With one of our four dimensional rocket tubes we shall be able to travel into hyperspace as far as we please, and then, by shooting discharge through the other tube we can just as easily direct our flyer back to three dimensional space.

"You already have some idea of the main purpose behind all this. My object is to use our four dimensional steering apparatus to release us quickly from the grip of gravitation when we want to escape from the Earth's pull. On the other hand, we can always return to three-dimensional space and to the gravitational fields of the Earth or moon whenever such attractive forces will be of any use to us. Is that all clear?"

"I—I—guess so," was Berglin's hesitating response.

CHAPTER FOUR
The Space Flyer Is Named

IN addition to the four-dimensional steering device, our space flyer had another unique and distinctive feature, namely the external lubricating system. This was simply a mechanical device for beating lubricating oil into millions of tiny bubbles and distributing them through small tubes to the exterior of the machine. By imposing rolling, oily contacts between the air and the outside surface of the flyer, this system cut down atmospheric resistance substantially and made it possible to travel through the Earth's gaseous envelope at speeds, which would otherwise have produced a terrific amount of friction and heat—more than sufficient to annihilate any conveyance which was not protected by this lubricating envelope.

The cabin, of course, had double walls, heavily insulated.

As our task neared completion I began to cudgel my brains for a fitting name with which to christen our mechanical baby. The only cognomens I could think of were either too trite or too commonplace-names like "The Hyphen" because it was to join the moon and the Earth. *"Excelsior"* and *"The Spirit of Luna"* were discarded because they were too reminiscent of other aircraft, which had won fame in bygone days.

One morning I entered the hangar to discover that the name question had been settled without any help from me. Under the direction of Professor Banning, a painter was just putting the finishing touches to the word: "A M U N D S E N."

"What do you think of it?" the Professor asked me.

"It certainly is an appropriate name. If Amundsen were alive today, he'd be just the kind of man who would endorse a trip like the one we are going to take. No one who ever lived is more worthy of the honor of having your flyer named after him."

"That's the way I feel about it, I consider your famous countryman as the greatest of explorers—the man who discovered the north magnetic pole and the northwest passage, the first man to reach the South Pole, and the only man so far who has seen one pole and has visited the other one in person. But great as these achievements were, they fade into insignificance when compared to his final voyage into the great unknown, when he sacrificed his life in an effort to save a man whom he considered an enemy.

"That's why I am proud to name my flyer after Captain Roald Amundsen!"

CHAPTER FIVE
The Trial Flight

WHEN the *Amundsen* was almost completed, Professor Banning sent a wire to Colonel Berglin, who was then in Washington attending to his engrossing duties as head of the newly created department of aviation. Two days later Berglin arrived in his famous "air office."

It was decided first to test the *Amundsen* as a terrestrial flyer without making any attempt to leave the Earth's atmosphere or gravitational field. For this reason the four dimensional tubes were not to be used and it was not considered necessary for me to go along. Naturally I was on hand at the time scheduled for the trial flight and I observed the performance from the ground.

Professor Banning and Colonel Berglin entered the cabin and a few minutes later I heard a hissing sound, which told me that the rocket tubes were in operation. Evidently only a small amount of power was being used at the start. For several minutes the machine taxied around the field making a series of short low hops. Suddenly, without warning, there shot out of the rear a blast which sent up a great cloud of gravel, and the *Amundsen* leaped heavenward, at a terrific pace. In a few seconds it had reached an altitude of several thousand feet. It then began the most preposterous series of stunts that have ever been witnessed. It looped and it sideslipped; it rolled like a barrel and spun like a top. It ended up by flying upside down in a wide circle, while at the same time it fluttered like a falling leaf, losing altitude at a terrific rate.

I stood rooted to the spot in helpless horror! A terrible accident was about to occur before my eyes! So certain did this seem that I even had a momentary mental picture of the mangled bodies of my two dearest friends lying amid a nightmare vision of twisted steel.

I closed my eyes to shut out the gruesome sight. I held my breath and waited for the crash.

Nothing happened.

When I could stand the strain no longer, I opened my eyes. At first I could see nothing in the air and I concluded that in some inexplicable way the flyer had crashed without making a noise loud enough for me to hear.

But the handful of mechanics and airdrome officials who had gathered to watch the hop-off were all still looking at the sky.

With the aid of my field glasses I was able to discern the unique outlines of the *Amundsen,* sailing majestically upward and onward and apparently under perfect control.

I learned later that the erratic behavior of the *Amundsen* had been due to a slight defect in the adjustment of the mechanism for controlling the blasts through the eight steering tubes. The wild antics performed in midair were due to Berglin's attempts to find out what was wrong. He had finally located the trouble just in time to prevent a serious crash. By manipulating the joystick carefully in such a way as to make allowance for the defective adjustment, he had gotten the flyer under control and thereafter had no difficulty in making it do just what he wished.

After climbing to an altitude of over 50,000 feet in about ten minutes, Berglin coasted back to Earth at an abrupt angle. He could easily have gone higher, but that was hardly necessary since the performance of the *Amundsen* was sufficient to prove its fitness for its destined task.

On the downward journey the *Amundsen* approached the airdrome at a tremendous speed. It looked as if it could never land without being carried off the field by its own momentum. But when it was about five hundred feet from the ground, the forward pointing rocket tubes were brought into play. With marvelous rapidity the acceleration was diminished until the machine seemed almost to be suspended in mid air. Then it slowly floated down to Earth, settling as softly and noiselessly as a dandelion seed.

CHAPTER SIX
Off for the Moon

THE trouble with the *Amundsen's* steering mechanism was quickly remedied and a second trial flight demonstrated that the space flyer was thoroughly fit and ready for its crucial journey to the moon. At this time we also tried out the four dimensional steering device and it proved to be a wonderful success.

After everything had been made ready for the hop-off, Banning timed our departure so that it came when the moon was in its first quarter and was trailing the Earth in its journey around the sun. While this was not an essential condition of a successful flight to the moon, it made possible a substantial increase in our speed and a saving of fuel, since it enabled us to take advantage of the motion of the moon itself.

Except for the unusual care, which we took in checking over all our supplies and equipment, our take-off, was uneventful. Only our assistants and most intimate friends knew about our plans. In order to avoid publicity, we embarked in the small hours of the morning.

The instant we were off the ground, Berglin pointed the nose of our flyer upward at a steep angle and so rapidly did we climb that it took us but a few minutes to reach the highly rarefied portions of the Earth's atmosphere.

We were then ready to execute our famous hairpin turn, by means of which we borrowed a tremendous amount of momentum from mother Earth and at the same time took advantage of the speed with which the moon was hurtling through space in its journey around the sun.

Following Professor Banning's instructions, Berglin headed the flyer in such a way that it pointed in the same direction that the Earth itself was moving.

"Now give her a shot into hyperspace!" the Professor commanded, and I directed a current of exploding radatomite through one of the four dimensional rocket tubes.

Under the circumstances one might naturally expect a violent shock or jar but nothing of the sort happened. Instead we experienced a most peculiar twisting sensation like the skidding of an automobile on a slippery pavement.

For a few seconds we were projected into hyperspace, then Professor Banning said, "By this time we must be pretty well out of the gravitational field of the Earth. So you may as well turn the ship about, Colonel."

Following these orders, Berglin operated the rocket tubes in such a way as to make a wide U turn, bringing the nose of the flyer around so it pointed straight toward the moon and in the opposite direction from that in which the Earth was moving.

Perhaps an analogy will make the purpose of this maneuver clear.

Imagine a boy on skates being towed across a frozen lake by a horse traveling at the rate of twenty miles per hour, and being followed at some distance by his dog who is running at exactly the same speed as the horse; that is, twenty miles per hour.

The boy lets go of the towrope and, without making any effort to increase his speed, executes a hairpin turn so that he faces toward the dog. It is apparent that he will now be approaching the dog at a speed equal to the dog's velocity added to the original velocity of the horse, or with a total speed of forty miles per hour. Naturally he will lose some momentum in making the turn and also in coasting after the turn, but it will require only a relatively small amount of effort on his part to make up for this loss of momentum.

In our case, the Earth took the part of the horse, the space flyer was the boy, and the moon was the dog. The towrope, which fastened us to the Earth, was the force of gravitation. When we projected ourselves into hyperspace, we virtually cut the rope. After making the hairpin turn, we found ourselves speeding toward the moon while the satellite was rushing toward us. And since, by that time, we had reached the interplanetary space where there was no atmosphere to create friction or resistance, our momentum was practically equal to that with which the Earth was traveling around the sun.

"You may as well shut off the power now," Professor Banning directed. "We can easily coast most of the way. With no atmosphere to retard us, our present momentum should continue indefinitely. Suppose we make a rough estimate of our velocity. At the time we shot off into hyperspace our flyer was making a speed of about a thousand miles an hour. We were also traveling with the Earth in its orbital flight at the rate of approximately 66,600 miles per hour. That makes our total speed pretty close to 67,600 miles per hour. At the same time the moon is now rushing toward us a trifle faster than 66,600 miles per hour. We are therefore approaching the moon at the rate of something like 134,000 miles per hour, so we ought to be able to cover the 238,851 miles between us and the moon in less than two hours.

"Of course we could increase our speed still more by using our rocket tubes, but I consider our present rate of progress quite satisfactory. What do you boys think about it?"

"Suits me," said Berglin.

"Me, too," I chimed in.

As we had hopped off when it was still dark, we were in the shadow of the Earth for several minutes. It wasn't long, however, before one edge of the huge spheroid behind us became visible, and a moment later the great blazing orb of the sun peeped at us from behind the Earth.

The most spectacular phenomenon of the aurora borealis was insignificant compared with the marvelous play of light and colors which we witnessed as the sunlight filtered to us through the Earth's atmospheric envelope. Almost in the twinkling of an eye the sun had leaped clear of the concealing globe and its corona became clearly visible. Old Sol looked as if it had suddenly increased enormously in size. Instead of appearing to be round, it was irregular in size with great jagged tongues of flame shooting out in all directions.

The stars, too, seemed much bigger, brighter, and more numerous than when observed from the surface of the Earth. They shone with marvelous splendor.

It wasn't long before we began to notice the effects of being relieved from the gravitational attraction of the Earth.

We learned that it was safer to remain seated and to avoid any sudden motion. Once, when I forgot myself and took a quick step in the direction of the water olla or cooler, I shot up into the air like a toy balloon and bumped my head against the roof of the cabin.

After assuring himself that I was not hurt, Professor Banning said, "Here, try these on."

He handed me a pair of sandals made of iron. "Strap them on so the iron parts are under the soles of your shoes," he explained. "They are magnetized so they will stick to the steel wall of the flyer."

I strapped on the sandals and found to my astonishment that I could walk like a fly, up the walls and along the ceiling, with my head pointing downward.

All three of us noticed peculiar physiological and psychological effects, which Professor Banning told us, were due largely to the sudden removal of the Earth's gravitation to which our bodies had always been accustomed.

A feeling of nausea, like that which a person experiences when he is in a rapidly descending elevator, was one of the most noticeable symptoms. We were also troubled with severe headaches, which were no doubt due to expansion of our brains accompanying the removal of gravitational pressure.

Mentally we were all three afflicted with the most excruciating pangs of homesickness. There was something about being away out there in space, thousands of miles from any other solid substance, that made me feel desperately lonesome and melancholy, in spite of the fact that there was no one on Earth for whom I cared anywhere near as much as for the two friends who were but a few feet away from me, where I could look at them and converse with them at will. But the marvelous power, which the human body has to adapt itself to all sorts of unfamiliar conditions soon, enabled us to overcome our disagreeable sensations and mental reactions.

It wasn't long before the half moon ahead of us loomed up with such gigantic proportions that we realized it was time to prepare for a landing.

CHAPTER SEVEN
We Alight on the Moon

WHEN it is recalled that we were approaching the moon at the terrific speed of about 134,000 miles per hour, the difficulty of alighting without annihilating ourselves and our machine becomes apparent.

We could, of course, diminish our speed somewhat by discharging our rocket tubes in a direction opposite to that in which we were moving, but it would have been necessary to start this braking process when we were only half way to our destination, and this would have consumed a great amount of time as well as fuel.

We employed the same principle that a man uses when he boards a moving streetcar. Everybody knows, that if a person should run toward an approaching vehicle and attempt to hop aboard it as it rushes by, he would be certain to meet with an accident. On the other hand, if he moves as fast as he can in the same direction as the streetcar is traveling, he has a much better chance to board it safely.

As we dashed toward the moon, Berglin steered with the rocket devices in such a way that we made a wide horseshoe turn around the moon. We were then traveling in the same direction as the moon and at approximately the same speed. I then sent a charge through the four-dimensional rocket tube, which brought us into the gravitational field of the moon. This caused an increase in our velocity.

Within a few moments we found ourselves flying swiftly at an altitude of about ten thousand feet above the surface of the moon.

It was then that we began to appreciate the marvelous beauty of the Earth's fair satellite. Having gazed at the weird lunar landscapes, gorgeous and cataclysmic in their grandeur, we could easily understand why a noted scientist, whose knowledge of the moon was confined to telescopic observation, made the statement that the Earth's satellite is the greatest scenic resort in the Solar System and in many ways the most fascinating object within the confines of the (telescopically) visible Universe.

Though we needed no explanations to appreciate the incomparable beauties of the panorama which quickly unfolded itself beneath us, Berglin and I felt doubly fortunate in being personally conducted by a man of Professor Banning's accurate and profound learning. There seemed to be no subject, scientific or otherwise, of which Professor Banning did not have a thorough and masterful knowledge. He certainly was well informed regarding the moon.

"Do you know, boys," he told us, "it just happens that we have approached the moon from the region nearest to its south pole. Notice that marvelous chain of mountains over there. They are the Leibnitz Mountains. Neison figured out that one of those summits has an elevation of nearly thirty-six thousand feet, which is about seven thousand feet higher than Mount Everest, the highest peak on the Earth!

"When you consider that the moon itself is only one forty-ninth as large as the Earth and has less than one-fourteenth of the surface area of our planet, you can appreciate how big these mountains are in proportion to the size of the sphere on which they are located. If the moon were expanded to the size of the Earth, the Liebnitz Mountains would be at least seventy-nine thousand, two-hundred feet, or more than fifteen miles high!

"Now if you'll look off to the left a little you'll see one of the most interesting sights in the Universe. Those are the Doerfel Mountains. Flammarion called them and the Leibnitz Mountains "the mountains of eternal light." Notice that the Doerfel Mountains are now on the part of the moon which is not illuminated by the sun, yet the peaks are so high above the surface that they actually jut out of the shadow and into the sunlit portion of space above the moon."

With amazement and admiration approaching awe, Berglin and I silently observed these marvels, which never before had been beheld at such close range by human eyes. The dazzling beauty of the brilliant, illuminated peaks, as contrasted with the Stygian darkness of the main bodies of the mountains, was accentuated by the fact that they were covered with hoarfrost which sparkled and glittered like myriad of gigantic diamonds.

Finally Berglin broke the spell with, "Well, Professor, where shall we land?"

"Do you see that circular formation straight ahead and a little to the right? That is a crater or ring mountain, and is known as Clavius. The space inside the crater ought to be both level and solid; in fact it should make an ideal landing field."

Within a short time we were circling over the crater and Berglin guided the *Amundsen* so skillfully that we alighted safely without the suggestion of a jar or bump almost in the exact center of the ring.

Then an amazing thing happened. When we looked out of the windows expecting to find a ring of mountains surrounding us on all sides, we were astonished to discover that the walls had disappeared completely, and, except for a few peaks which rose from the surface of the interior and which were clearly visible, we found ourselves in what looked like a vast plain extending to the horizon in all directions.

"What in the world has happened to our ring of mountains!" I exclaimed.

"That's easily explained," Professor Banning responded. "The space inside this crater is no less than one hundred and forty miles in diameter. The wall to the west of us is seventeen thousand, three hundred feet high, and the east wall is over three miles high. That sounds as if they ought to be big enough to be seen even at a distance of seventy miles, but the fact of the matter is that, because of the curvature of the moon's surface, the peaks of our mountain walls are actually below the horizon."

"Shall we put on our suits and take a stroll around?" I suggested.

"Not yet," the Professor decided. "I believe we can see all there is to see here without getting outside the space flyer. Suppose we taxi for a few miles toward the west until we come in sight of the mountain wall."

Berglin turned on enough power through the rear rocket tubes to set us in motion and soon we were spinning along in a series of long hops at a speed of about seventy miles per hour.

In about half an hour the peaks of the crater rim hove in sight and a little while later we were able to distinguish the entire wall of hills ahead of us.

"Not much use in trying to do any exploring here," the Professor muttered. "It's just as I expected. Although these ring mountains slope very gently on the outside, their sides are rather steep on the inside. I'd estimate that those hills ahead of us have an inclination of at least forty-five degrees and that's too steep to climb in comfort, even on the moon. I guess we may as well fly out of this crater and land in some place outside where we'll have a better chance to do some real exploring."

"How about flying around to the other side of the moon—the half that is never seen from the Earth!" I exclaimed eagerly.

"Plenty of time for that later. What I'd like to do first is to see if we can't solve some of the puzzles on this side of the moon—puzzles that have baffled the selenographers for the past hundred years."

CHAPTER EIGHT
Caught in a Lunar Trap

"ONE of the first things I'd like to settle," Professor Banning continued, "is the nature and composition of the streaks or rays which no one has yet succeeded in explaining satisfactorily. A large number of these streaks radiate from the ring mountain Tycho, which is not far from here. Suppose we take to the air—or rather to the ether and see how these streaks look from above at close range."

Pursuant to the Professor's suggestion, Berglin "gave the gun" to our rocket tubes and, without the slightest difficulty, our flyer rose and soared over the walls of Clavius. Tycho is about one hundred and fifty miles due north of Clavius, and it took but a few minutes to cover this distance.

"Shall we set her down?" Berglin asked.

"Not yet," Banning instructed. "Let us fly around for a while and get a bird's eye view of this formation."

It was truly a remarkable sight! Tycho reminded me of a colossal hub from which radiated over a hundred of the remarkable streaks with almost as much regularity as the spokes of a gigantic wheel. There were however a considerable amount of variation in the thickness and length of the rays. The largest of them extended in a northwesterly direction in a line, which was remarkably straight. The marvelous thing about it was that it seemed to disregard utterly every obstacle, which lay in its path.

Not far from Tycho we saw a ring mountain of considerable size which Professor Banning told us was called Saussure. It did not deflect the large ray in the slightest degree. Up one side of the southerly wall the streak climbed—down the other side, across the interior, up to the summit of the north wall and down to the plain, along which it could be seen, stretching out to the horizon.

Continuing in a northwesterly direction, we gained altitude, so that more and more of the ray came into view. We followed its path to the place where it crossed a large depression which we learned was known as the Sea of Serenity. This so-called sea did not contain any water, of course, although the greenish, silvery luster of its surface created a remarkable illusion that suggested a lake of mercury.

Despite the brightness of the sea itself, the great ray, cutting directly through the middle of it, stood out with dazzling brilliancy.

"That ray is about ten miles wide and over 2,000 miles long," Banning informed us. "It starts at Tycho near the south pole and terminates at the Sea of Cold close to the opposite edge of the moon. The most astonishing thing is its straightness. It's just as if some superior being had laid a flexible rule along the surface of the moon and had traced the ray with ink made of diamond dust."

"It sure does!" was my banal response to my friend's beautiful flight of fancy.

"What do you suppose that streak is made of?" Colonel Berglin asked Banning.

"That's one thing I hope to find out. One of the favorite theories is that these rays started as cracks formed in the surface of the moon when it cooled from a molten state.

This is supported by the fact when a glass sphere is heated and then cooled suddenly by plunging it into cold water, cracks are formed which are very similar in character to the rays on the moon."

This prompted a remark from Berglin: "But if they are just cracks, they would be like crevasses or canyons. They look to me as if they are flush with the surface."

"That's true, and the logical explanation is that the cracks were subsequently filled in with some substance which reflects the light. Suppose for instance that at one time there were rivers and lakes on the moon, which is not only possible, but very probable. Suppose that water, which had passed over rocks containing soluble minerals, had poured into the cracks in the surface of the moon. The water would be evaporated by the heat, leaving the mineral matter deposited in the cracks. After a while the cracks would be filled to the top with material, which would be entirely different from the soil around it.

"Another possibility is that the cracks became filled with molten metal which oozed up from within the moon and subsequently cooled and solidified.

"But now that we are here, what's the use of supposing any more? Let's go down there and find out definitely."

We picked a spot in the Sea of Serenity, which looked like an ideal place to land. It was as level as a baseball diamond and was covered with a fine, silvery dust, Berglin made a perfect landing, setting the flyer down gently and accurately.

Then something horrible—something totally unexpected—happened. Like a scuttled ship plunging into the depths of the ocean our flyer sank into that treacherous sea of fine dust. Quickly the light was blotted out as the dust covered our windows and engulfed us. Down, down we went until we must have been at least thirty feet beneath the surface. When we finally came to a standstill we had the feeling of being supported on a cushion rather than resting on firm ground.

I leaped to my feet and as I did so the impact of my shoes against the floor sent us down a few feet further.

"My God!" I cried in a voice, which must have reverberated with terror. "We're buried alive! What a horrible death! Oh, why did we come on this trip?"

Neither Berglin nor Banning displayed any signs of fear or other emotion, which made me feel rather ashamed of myself after the first shock of fright had passed off.

"Don't get excited," Banning admonished me. "And, above everything, don't lose your head. We've all been in worse scrapes than this before and we've gotten out of them. Just make up your mind that we are going to get out of this one."

"O.K., Professor, I'll try to get a grip on myself," I assured him. "Sorry I lost control of myself. But when I felt myself sinking, sinking—it made me feel so helpless that—"

"I understand," the Professor said in his most kindly tones. "And now suppose we plan a way to get out of this hole."

"I don't see any reason why we can't fly out," Berglin volunteered. "If this dust is so fine and so loose that it let us sink this far, it ought to be just as easy for us to get through it on the way out."

"That sounds reasonable enough," said Banning. "It won't hurt to try, anyway."

Berglin took his place at the controls and started the rocket motor. Cautiously he directed a blast through the rear tubes. At first we sank a few feet further. This was probably caused by the loosening of the dust behind and beneath us. But as Berglin increased the power, the *Amundsen* began to move forward and upward, steadily gaining momentum until it suddenly burst into the full glare of the lunar sunshine.

"Hurrah!" I yelled. "It worked! We're out of it! We're safe! And now, for the love of mud, let's steer clear out of those blankety-blank seas."

"Where do we go now?" This from Berglin.

"Turn south," was Banning's laconic order.

After we had flown in the direction indicated for a few minutes, Banning said, "See the ring mountain just ahead? That is Rheitas. I think we'll be able to land safely in that level place just to the west of it."

Following these instructions, Berglin set the flyer down and I heaved a sigh of relief as I felt the machine come to rest on solid ground.

"This is almost the center of the lunar disk which is visible from the Earth," Professor Banning remarked. "It's a good place to take possession."

"Take possession?" I exclaimed. "What do you mean by that?"

"I mean that I hold a commission which authorizes me to take possession of the moon in the name of the Government of the United States of America!"

CHAPTER NINE
Taking Possession of the Moon

WHEN Professor Banning announced his intention of taking possession of the moon in the name of the United States Government, I thought at first he was joking, but he soon convinced me that he was in dead earnest. To me it seemed ridiculous, a futile thing to do—for of what use could a dead, barren, uninviting world like the moon be to any nation?

Knowing Professor Banning as well as I did, however, I felt positive that there must be some strong valid reason behind his seemingly useless act, so I said nothing.

Well, my boy," Banning said to me in a jubilant voice, "at last the time has come to try out our space suits! What do you say if we go for a little lunar hike?"

"O.K., Chief," I replied. I tried to speak in a matter-of-fact way, but I am afraid I betrayed the fact that I was suffering a bit from "buck fever." Somehow or other, the prospect of meandering around through the weird, ghostly landscape of the moon was anything but attractive to me. There was nothing to do but go through with it, however, and I would rather have perished on the spot than to have either Banning or Berglin know that I was afraid.

For several reasons, only two space suits were included in the equipment of the *Amundsen*. One reason was that they took up considerable room, and space was naturally at a premium. Professor Banning had also decided that at no time during our trip would be advisable for all three of us to leave the *Amundsen*. Since Berglin was the official pilot of our flyer it was only natural that he should be the one chosen to stay with the ship, at least during our first trial.

The space suit invented by Professor Banning was built on the principle of a pneumatic tire—in fact, the major portion of it was constructed by a prominent manufacturer of automobile tires. The exterior of the suit corresponded to the casing of a tire. It looked for all the world like a well known trade character used in the advertising of a pneumatic tire concern—the Michelin—a man composed of tires cemented together by their sides, so as to give the appearance of a corrugated surface.

These outer walls of the suit were built with extra strength, like the heavy duty cord tires used on large motor trucks. On the inside was a lining of flexible rubber, similar to that used in making inner tubes. These linings were cemented to the collar of the suit with an airtight joint. To the shoulder plate was attached a heavy glass globe which could be screwed on like the helmet of a diver's costume.

A knapsack fastened to the back of the suit contained, in very compact space, a tank of oxygen, a storage battery, miniature radio sending and receiving sets, a cooling device, and an air-purifying system.

The waistline was encompassed by a wide leather belt fitted with hooks to which were attached a hammer, a drill, a small pickaxe and a large trowel. The belt also contained several pockets, which were designed to receive samples of soil and rock to be collected during our exploration.

Before getting into our space suits, Professor Banning and I each donned a union suit made of wool. It had a tight-fitting hood, which covered the head and lower part of face, leaving only the eyes and nose exposed. Into this hood were built the earphones and also the microphone of the radio apparatus.

The fabric of the undergarment was interwoven with fine electric wires, like an electric heating pad. Connected with the suit was a cable containing the wires for the heating device, the radio sets and also the apparatus for controlling the air supply and the cooling system. This cable was plugged into the knapsack through an outlet on the inside of the collar.

Having thus prepared ourselves we put on the space suits and Berglin screwed our glass helmets in place. When thus equipped, we each represented a complete plant for existing independently in the airless space surrounding the moon.

The radio enabled us to communicate with each other and also kept us in close touch with Berglin, who had a corresponding outfit inside the *Amundsen*. With our oxygen tanks and our air-purifying apparatus we could breathe comfortably for at least ten hours. If the temperature became uncomfortably low, we could turn on the electric heat—if we found it too hot we could keep ourselves cool by means of our refrigerating device.

For grasping tools, picking up objects, and similar acts, Banning had provided a pair of very ingenious mechanical hands, which were operated by grips inside the arms of the suits.

Our airlock was just large enough for one person at a time, Professor Banning insisted on being the first one to use it. Carrying a stick wrapped in bunting, he entered the narrow chamber and closed the door. A few minutes later we heard the grating of the outer door and soon the grotesque form of the professor clad in his outlandish costume came into a position where we could see him through the window of the flyer.

With an unmistakable gesture, he beckoned me to follow him. As familiar as I was with the operation of the radio device, I was so startled that I nearly jumped out of my space suit when I heard his voice in my ear say, "Come on, my boy! It's fine out here!"

I turned the valve, which allowed air from the flyer to pass into the airlock. Then I opened the door and stepped into the small closet. Fastening the door tightly, I pressed the button, which operated the air pump. When the indicator pointed to zero, I unfastened the outer door and stepped awkwardly out upon the surface of the moon.

I had expected to feel a series of peculiar sensations, but except for a feeling of buoyant freedom, I felt just about the same as I did when I was inside the *Amundsen*. But when I attempted to stride forth at my usual hiking speed, I suddenly discovered that I was in a new and different environment.

The step, which would ordinarily have carried me a yard or so, was more like the leap of a kangaroo. It sent me into the air in a rainbow loop, which was fully ten feet high and fifteen feet long. It was so unexpected that I wasn't prepared to make a safe landing. My body pitched forward and I landed in a heap, tumbling over and over on the ground before I recovered by balance.

Banning waited until he saw me scramble to my feet. Then, after he had apparently assured himself that I was not hurt, he laughed uproariously. Thanks to the radio, I got full benefit of his hilarity.

In my earphones I heard the Professor's voice say, "Excuse me for laughing, but you looked so comical that I couldn't help it. Your tumble didn't hurt you, did it ?"

"Not a bit," I assured him. "I don't blame you for laughing. Guess I did look funny. I feel almost as if I was inside a balloon."

"You'll soon get used to it. But until you do you'd better move very slowly and carefully. Don't forget that the force of gravitation here on the moon is only about one-sixth as strong as it is on the Earth."

"It didn't take me long to find that out," was my reply.

With awkward, shambling steps, Banning walked to a spot where there were a number of rocks lying loose on the ground. He gathered together a score of these stones and built a small monument. Then he unwound the bunting from his staff, revealing an American flag, which he placed in such a way that the stones held the pole upright. There was not the slightest vestige of a breeze on the airless moon, of course, so the flag hung listlessly from the staff.

The sight of our national emblem amid the incongruous surroundings of the lunar landscape sent an incomparable thrill of patriotism through me and made my spine tingle. I brought my heels together and raised my mechanical hand to my forehead in a grotesque, but none the less respectful salute. When I took a quick glance over my shoulder, I could see Berglin standing at attention with his face toward the flag.

Professor Banning also saluted, as he pronounced these words in an impressive voice: "I hereby take possession of this land and all the remainder of the land on the moon in the name of the United States of America."

CHAPTER TEN
The Explosion

AFTER completing the formality of taking possession of the moon, Professor Banning walked westward toward the great ray, which was but a short distance from the place where we had alighted. Cautiously and awkwardly, I shuffled after him. When he arrived at the edge of the glittering streak, he detached from his belt a drill. Then he squatted down, holding the drill in an upright position.

"Take your hammer," he instructed me, "and see if you can hit the head of this drill without cracking the fingers of my mechanical hand."

Following his orders I grasped my hammer and succeeded in striking the drill squarely with the first blow. It seemed to have very little effect. The hammer felt extremely light, which was due of course to the small amount of attraction, which the moon exerted, on it. After what seemed like over an hour of feeble tapping, I managed to sink the drill down about ten inches.

To my great relief, Banning said, "I think that's deep enough." Fumbling in one of his voluminous pockets he drew forth a small sack. From it he poured into the hole a handful of powder, which I recognized as radatomite, the same explosive as we used for fuel in operating the *Amundsen*.

From his belt he removed a coil of wire with a small cylindrical object attached to one end. This he placed over the charge of explosive. Filling the hole with loose dirt, he tapped it down with the upper end or head of the drill.

Then he said to me, "You see that boulder over there? I mean the one that's about six feet in diameter. Go and fetch it here for me, will you please?"

"You want me to fetch that enormous rock for you?" I exclaimed. "Say, what do you think I am, Hercules, Samson, or some other professional strong man!"

"You don't need to be a Samson to lift that stone. Suppose you go over there and try."

I walked up to the boulder and managed to get a good grip on it with my mechanical fingers. Then I braced myself and gave a mighty heave. Much to my astonishment it came up so easily that it threw me off my balance and I sat down, with the great rock resting on my lap. Had an earthly stone as large as that fallen on me, I would have been seriously crushed beneath the weight of it, but the lunar rock rested on my legs as lightly as if it had been made of cork.

Scrambling to my feet again, I had no difficulty in lifting the rock and carrying it to Banning. He rolled it into a position directly over the hole containing the charge of explosive. Then he walked away, uncoiling the wire behind him.

I stepped back a few yards and stopped to watch, but the Professor continued to put more and more distance between himself and the charge. "Better come over here," he cautioned me. "That's liable to make things fly for some distance."

It was fortunate for me that I heeded his warning.

Banning exploded the charge by making an electrical connection with the storage battery, which was part of his equipment.

Expecting a loud detonation, I stood with my mouth open. But not even the faintest ghost of a sound reached my waiting ears. Amid a deathly silence the ground seemed to burst open, sending a geyser of glittering lumps high into the air. The huge boulder shot into the air as if it were a toy balloon. But instead of dropping like a similar object would fall on the Earth, it seemed to float down, slowly and leisurely. The fragments torn from the great ray behaved in a similar manner, of course. It was fortunate for us that they did descend with moderated velocity, for several of them came so close to us that we had to move quickly to get out of their way. It would have been rather difficult, if not impossible, to dodge missiles like that, had they dropped upon us with the speed of falling bodies on the Earth.

His pedagogic training coming to the surface, Professor Banning took this occasion to point out the scientific aspects of this phenomenon.

"You see," he explained. "The effect of that explosion was a great deal greater here than it would have been on Earth, because there was a smaller amount of resistance to overcome. The fragments were thrown about six times as far as they would have been back home. This is due to the fact that the force of gravitation is only about one-sixth as strong here as it is on Earth. For the same reason, when the pieces started to come down, they fell at a much slower speed than they would have done on our terrestrial sphere.

"The Earth's gravitation makes a freely falling body drop a little over sixteen feet the first second. On the moon, the same object would fall only two feet and eight inches during the first second."

"But how come I didn't hear the explosion?" I asked. "You ought to be able to answer that if you just use your brains. You know, of course, that sound can only travel through a solid, a liquid, or a gas. It will not penetrate a vacuum. The reason you didn't hear any sound was that there was nothing between you and the explosion which was capable of transmitting sound."

"But how about your voice coming to me over the radio?"

"That's altogether different. Radio waves don't need a material conductor. They travel through the ether and there's plenty of ether even on the moon."

"Why, of course, I know that. I just didn't use my head—that's all."

The Professor began to coil the wire.

"Suppose we gather up some of these samples we blew loose," he suggested.

Following Banning's example I picked up a few fragments of the material torn from the great ray. It was easy to recognize them by their silvery, metallic luster.

This accomplished, I asked, "Now, what do we do, Professor?"

"Do you see that ring mountain off there to your left? That is Rheitas. Now that we are here we may as well go over and take a look at it."

"O.K., Professor," I agreed, and started to walk in the direction which he had indicated.

"Hey, there!" He called after me. "Where are you going?"

"I'm going to hike over to that ring mountain."

"Hiking over there? Do you realize that it's nearly a hundred miles from here?"

"A hundred miles from here? Why, it looks as if it's only a mile or two away."

"You must remember that things look altogether different here on the moon. The reason that crater looks so close is that there is no atmosphere between us and it. On Earth we judge distances by the relative size of familiar objects and also by the clearness or haziness of the images cast on our retinas. Here the distant objects are nearly as clearly visible as those that are close by. Furthermore, we can only guess at the real size of distant objects and for that reason we can not make comparisons with any degree of accuracy.

"Of course, you could walk over there if you insist. With practice you ought to be able to travel pretty fast—say twenty miles an hour—so it will take you only about five hours to get there. But, for my part, I believe I'll have Berglin taxi me over there. No use exerting myself unnecessarily."

"Count me in on the taxi party, too," I said. "Hiking a hundred miles all by myself doesn't exactly appeal to me, even if I am a much faster walker up here than I ever dreamed I could be."

CHAPTER ELEVEN
A Perilous Hike

IN turn, Professor Banning and I entered the *Amundsen* through the airlock. Since the trip was to be a short one, we did not remove our space suits. It took but a few minutes for Berglin to cover the hundred miles that separated us from our objective. Once more the two of us emerged from the space flyer and strolled across the surface of the moon.

As the Professor had anticipated, we found that the external slopes of the ring mountain were not at all steep. I estimated the grade to be approximately five per cent. On the other hand, the interior walls were quite precipitous, ranging from twenty-five to fifty percent, in grade.

By this time we had become accustomed enough to our new environment so that we could move along at a pretty brisk pace, covering the ground in a series of long leaps. Up the gently sloping sides of Rheitas we hopped until we stood on the rim of the crater.

Here a marvelous sight met our eyes. Rheitas was by no means large compared with some of the other ring mountains. When compared with any similar formation on Earth, however, it was a veritable giant.

"This crater is about twenty miles across," Professor Banning elucidated. "Just how big this is, can be estimated by comparing it with the largest crater rings on the Earth, of which there are only three, which can boast a diameter as great as fifteen miles. They are Aso San in Japan, Lake Bourbon on the Island of Luzon in the Philippines, and a crater in northern Kamchatka. There are several large crater lakes in the United States, but not one of them is more than seven miles in diameter.

"Here on the moon there are many ring mountains that are over a hundred miles wide. The largest of all is Bailly. It measures about one hundred and eighty miles across."

As we stood on the rim of Rheitas, we could clearly distinguish the rugged and magnificent outlines of the opposite wall. In the center of the ring was a picturesque cone shaped mountain, which resembled a small volcano within a larger crater.

The colorings of the landscape were gorgeous. Never before had I seen such a riot of purple and green and magenta and orange as were splashed with reckless lavishness all over the incomparable scenery.

For some time we stood there feasting our eyes on this rare vista, then, half reluctantly, half eagerly, we retraced our steps.

Professor Banning was content with leaps of moderate length, covering, approximately ten yards at each step. But I, with the characteristic willfulness of youth, must attempt to establish a record for a lunar broad jump.

First I tried a few standing jumps and derived a tremendous amount of enjoyment from feeling myself soar up into the air for a height of ten feet or more. I expected to get a jolt when I landed but found that I alighted slowly and gently. This also was due to the fact that my body was being pulled down with only a fraction of the gravitational attraction on the Earth.

Next I attempted a hop, skip, and a jump, and found that I could leap both higher and further than from a standing start and still land without trouble. I then decided that I was ready to make a running broad jump that would far exceed the greatest accomplishments of the world's leading athletes. In this I succeeded with a vengeance.

Because of the difficulty in judging distance in the deceptive airless space surrounding the moon, I did not realize how close I was to the rim of a titanic gorge. When I reached the highest point of my lob, I found myself headed right into the maw of this horrible chasm, I tried to emulate the figure of a cat I once saw in a movie animated cartoon, which jumped off a high cliff and, changing its mind in mid-flight, pulled itself through the air and back to the top of the precipice.

With me, however, this scheme didn't seem to work very well. No matter how frantically I waved my arms and kicked my legs, I continued to drop with increasing acceleration—straight into the cleft.

Sometimes I marvel at the inconsistencies of the human mind—especially with respect to such qualities as pluck, nerve, and courage, I've heard of men who have repeatedly charged deadly machine-gun nests without flinching, but who whimpered like babies when threatened with the cold steel of a trench knife. There are those who have braved the perils of life aboard a submarine, who couldn't be hired to ride in an elevator.

Consider my own case, for instance. But a short time previous I had completely lost my nerve because I feared that we were to be buried alive inside our flyer. My fears turned out to be groundless. And now I was facing a far more serious danger and I wasn't scared in the least. The fact was that I actually joked about my predicament.

I was still dropping through space when I heard in my earphones the voice of Professor Banning calling my name.

"Are you hurt? Are you hurt?" he kept repeating in anxious tones.

"Not yet!" I yelled into my microphone as I plunged downward into the abyss. "I'm O.K., so far!"

I felt a sharp jolt as the nether portion of my space suit bumped against the steeply sloping walls of the canyon, and again I called out, "All right so far."

As I bounced down, now hitting the cliff, now hurtling through space, I clutched desperately at the precipitous rocks with my mechanical hands. Once I caught hold of something, but the force of my descent jerked my grip loose. However, this served to slacken my speed sufficiently so that I was able to hang to the next projection that came in my path. Finally I brought up with a thud and managed to clamber up upon an overhanging ledge.

You can understand that this feat was all the more difficult because it was performed in Stygian darkness. The instant I had passed over the edge of the canyon the light had been blotted out as suddenly and as completely as if the sun had been totally eclipsed. Considering the fact that the plain I had just left was bathed in dazzling sunshine, it seemed inconceivable that I could be so quickly plunged into darkness so dense that I literally could not see my mechanical fist when I held it in front of my helmet.

THE explanation was simple enough. Without any air, water vapor, or dust to diffuse the light of the sun there was a total absence of illumination in the shadow of the cliff. On the moon there was no light except in those places which were exposed to the direct rays of the sun, or to light reflected from some illuminated surface.

Again I heard Professor Banning's voice calling to me, "Are you all right?"

"I'm still O.K.," I radioed to him. "Right now I'm perched on a narrow ledge of rock somewhere between the top and the bottom of this God-forsaken hole."

"Stay right where you are!" he said. "We'll see what we can do about getting you out."

"Don't worry!" was my response. "I'll stay right where I am until you rescue me. You can absolutely depend on that."

I had hardly uttered these words before the ledge on which I was standing crumbled beneath me, and again I resumed my downward journey. Fortunately I didn't fall far enough to acquire much speed before I landed on a second ledge which felt larger and more secure than the other one.

As I crouched on that narrow projection shrouded in pitchy blackness I could sympathize thoroughly with Homer's fabled Cimmerians, whom he described as living in perpetual darkness. It was lucky for me that I had the assistance of a man as ingenious and as resourceful as Professor Banning. Simple and effective as his plan of rescue proved to be, few other men would have thought of it so quickly.

By way of encouragement and instruction he gave me this explanation via radio: "I have my pocket flashlight fastened to an electric cable. I am now going to lower this light over the edge of the cleft somewhere near the place where I saw you disappear. Watch for the light and let me know if I have it headed in the right direction."

I gazed upward and soon saw a tiny point of moving light. "I see it!" I cried. "But you'll miss me by several feet if you keep on lowering it from where you are."

"What direction shall I move it?" he asked.

"A little to the—" I was going to name one of the four points of the compass but when I tried to figure out my relative position with respect to the light, I found myself hopelessly confused. So I foolishly shouted, "Move it over this way."

The Professor must have understood my confusion for he moved the light and then said, "Did I move it closer that time?"

"Sure!" I yelled into my radio transmitter. "But you didn't move it far enough."

"How is that?" he said after he had altered his position.

"That's too far," I told him. "Back this way about six inches. There! Now it's directly overhead. Lower away!"

Closer and closer came that blessed speck of light until I could reach out and grasp the wire in my mechanical fist.

"I have hold of the cable," I called out. "Now what shall I do?"

"Wrap it around your body and fasten it securely, but in such a way that you can slip it off quickly."

"What are you going to do? Haul me out?"

"Why, certainly."

"Do you think this wire will hold the weight of my space suit with me inside it?"

"It ought to. If it doesn't, we'll have to figure out some other way."

"Figure out some other way!" I yelled. "Don't you realize that if you start pulling me out and this wire breaks there won't be enough of me left to do any figuring over?"

"But I'm telling you that the wire is plenty strong enough to bear your weight. Can't you take my word for that? At any rate, it's the strongest material we have on hand—so it's either the wire or nothing."

"All right," I consented. "But isn't there another danger? Suppose the rubbing of the cable against the edge of the rocks up there wears it so much that it breaks."

"I've thought of a way to avoid that," the Professor said, "I'll have Berglin pull you out with the aid of the *Amundsen.*"

At the time he made this statement I couldn't see what difference it would make in the wear on the cable whether I was pulled out by a person or a machine, but when I heard Banning's instructions to Berglin, I understood what he was driving at.

"I'm going to fasten the wire to the undercarriage of the flyer," I heard Banning say, "I want you to rise as slowly as you can. There are several hundred feet of slack, but you'll have to be awfully careful so that you do not bring the wire taut with a jerk."

This sounded like a risky thing to attempt but, thanks to Berglin's superb skill in manipulating the space flyer, it was preformed without mishap. Looking upward I saw the *Amundsen* circling around, gaining altitude by inches until, with an almost imperceptible tug, I was lifted gently into space. There I dangled, like a fish on the end of a line, while the flyer continued to climb.

With a suddenness that blinded me, my head popped from the Cimmerian darkness into the dazzling glare of the sunlight, I had sense enough to close my eyes and then open them very gradually.

When I was clear of the chasm, Berglin slowly descended until my feet were only a few inches from the ground. Then he dived in a steep spiral, thus relieving the tension on the cable. In this manner he deposited me softly and safely on the sunlit plain.

A moment later I had disengaged myself from the cable. By this time my eyes had become accustomed enough to the bright light so that I was able to make out the form of the

Professor in his space suit a short distance away. I also saw the *Amundsen* as Berglin set it down nearby.

Hastening to the beneficent protection of the space ship, I quickly entered the airlock and a few moments later was inside the cabin. This was rather inconsiderate of me, since it left the elderly professor the task of coiling the wire, which had been used in my rescue. I divested myself of my cumbersome garment and took several deep breaths of air, which seemed to taste much fresher than the atmosphere provided by the space suit.

When I glanced out of the window and saw Professor Banning laboring along with the heavy coil of wire, I felt very much ashamed and I hastened to apologize to him as soon as he appeared inside the *Amundsen*.

"Oh, that's all right," he said generously, "I understand your mental reactions perfectly. After the experience you had I could hardly expect you to lose any time in getting to a place, which you consider safer."

CHAPTER TWELVE
Our First Night On the Moon

WHEN I had sufficiently recovered from the effects of my harrowing experience, I remarked to the Professor, "That sure was some gully I got myself into. It must have taken millions of years for a cleft like that to be carved out."

"On the contrary," Banning corrected me. "It is more than likely that your little gully, as you call it, was carved out in a few seconds."

"I don't see how that could be possible."

"It wouldn't be, if it were done by water. But I think we can be absolutely certain that water had nothing to do with the making of that cleft. To be sure there might have been a considerable amount of moisture on the moon at some far distant time, but it would have been frozen solid throughout the lunar night, and would have been in the form of vapor during the periods of terrific heat when the sunlight was streaming down on this part of the moon. Under the circumstances, erosion such as takes place on the Earth could hardly dig out such a tremendous gash as that.

"I'm afraid that—even after your experience in exploring the inside of yonder cleft, you have no conception of its magnitude. It is twenty miles wide and a hundred and eighty-seven miles long."

"How in the world—or rather in the moon—can you say it is exactly so long and so wide?" I asked in amazement. "I don't remember seeing you measure it or even making an estimate of its size."

"The measuring was done a long time ago by selenographers who viewed the moon from the Earth through their telescopes. In some respects we know more about the geography of the moon than we do about certain portions of the Earth. It is a simple problem of triangulation to measure the length and width of any object on the moon. And, thanks to the clearness of the shadows, we can also measure the height of mountains and the depth of most of the valleys with equal exactness without leaving the Earth."

"But you said a moment ago that the valleys on the moon were not formed by water action, but were carved out in a few seconds. I suppose you mean that the moon must have been hit by another object."

"Precisely. Some authorities think it was caused by a comet hitting the moon, a glancing blow and plowing right through the surface. Other selenographers attribute it to a similar phenomenon caused by a meteor. I am inclined to hold to the meteor theory myself."

"Well, whatever it was that caused that gorge to be formed, I've seen all of it I care to, thank you," was my closing comment.

"What's our next move, Professor?" Berglin seemed impatient to keep going.

"I think the next thing for us to do is to get some rest. Do you realize, boys, that it is over thirty hours since we left the Earth and none of us has had a wink of sleep?"

It was true. What with the excitement occasioned by our incomparable adventures, combined with the brilliant sunlight and the slowness of the sun's passage across the sky, we had not realized how much time was elapsing.

The idea of taking a rest was decidedly welcome to me. Though I had not felt the least bit tired before, once the thought had been suggested to me I found myself overcome with profound weariness.

"Shall we turn in right here?" I asked.

"If you want to," the Professor replied. "But I think we will find it easier to sleep if we move over to the night section of the moon."

"What?" I cried. "Do you want us all to commit suicide?"

"What do you mean by suicide?"

"That's exactly what we would be doing if we tried to land the flyer in the dark. Believe me, I've been in the moon's darkness and I'm telling you that it's so dark down there that in comparison with it a lump of coal would look like a snowball."

"But you were in a shaded place. My idea was to land in the open but on a portion of the moon where the sun isn't shining."

"Well, if it's as dark as that in the shadow of a cliff, in the daytime, how much darker will it be at night?"

"Don't worry, we'll have plenty of light to land by. You seem to have forgotten our old friend the Earth will give us earthlight."

Instinctively I gazed up at the sky. Hanging there motionless—almost exactly in the zenith—was good old Mother Earth. Though we were still exposed to the brilliant light of the sun, the sky was jet black and was studded with myriad of stars. They seemed to be far more numerous and to shine with much greater brilliancy than when viewed from the Earth in their most brilliant display.

Our mother planet resembled the moon—but what a moon! Its diameter was four times as large as that of Luna as seen from the Earth. Our position was such that the Earth was in what might be called its last quarter. Only half of it was visible and the remaining portion of its disc was like a huge semi-circular hole cut out of the star-studded background of the sable sky.

The ice caps surrounding the north and south poles were very clearly visible as they reflected the light of the sun with sparkling brilliancy. It was rather difficult to distinguish the conformation of the continents because of the mantle of clouds that hung about the orb, but between patches of the clouds I was able to make out the outlines of the British Isles and of the Scandinavian Peninsula.

Professor Banning went on with his explanation: "When we get over to the dark side of the moon we'll find the country bathed in earthlight. The Earth, of course, has its phases, just like the moon. When the Earth is full, it reflects to the moon about thirteen times as much light as the full moon sends to the Earth. Even with only half the Earth illuminated as it is now, we will find that it is about six times as light as it is on a clear night on Earth when the full moon is directly overhead."

As usual, Professor Banning's predictions were fulfilled with amazing exactness. With Berglin at the controls we hopped off by daylight and within a short time we had flown into the region of lunar night.

If the scenery of the moon was magnificent in the sunlight's brilliant glare, it was incomparably beautiful in the soft, bluish light of the Earth. There was an abundance of illumination and we could easily distinguish even the small objects below us.

WITHOUT the slightest difficulty, Berglin set the *Amundsen* down in the center of the ring mountain, Eratosthenes. It was not until some time later that we learned the reason why Professor Banning had selected this particular spot for our camping ground on our first night on the moon.

Before retiring, Professor Banning took a reading of the thermometer, which was especially designed, for registering the temperature of the space outside the *Amundsen*. It was minus 137 degrees Centigrade. Reduced to the Fahrenheit scale this represented a temperature of 215 degrees below zero.

For purposes of comparison it may be of interest to mention here that subsequent reading made on the moon ranged from 240 degrees below zero Fahrenheit just after dawn to 218 degrees Fahrenheit at the lunar noon. It will be noted that this maximum temperature is six degrees higher than the boiling point of water at sea level on the Earth. In the airless space surrounding the moon, the small amount of water there would change almost instantly from ice to vapor.

In spite of the hollow walls of the *Amundsen* and the heavy insulation between them, the bitter cold of the lunar night soon began to make itself felt within the flyer and we were glad to make use of our electric heating equipment.

Without divesting ourselves of our clothing, we rolled ourselves in our blankets and lay down on our pneumatic mattresses. In a few minutes the labored breathing of my two companions told me that they had quickly fallen asleep, I, too, was physically fatigued, but my mind insisted on staying awake. This was probably due in large measure to the effects of my accident. Through a window in our portable home I could see the Earth, hanging there in space like half a gigantic melon. It filled me with the most excruciating pangs of lonesomeness and homesickness to behold my native planet away out there across that awful stretch of empty space.

It wasn't long, however, before my bodily weariness triumphed over my mental alertness. The subtle glue, of which Stevenson speaks, slipped beneath my eyelids and I fell into a sound slumber.

I awoke to gaze in open-mouthed astonishment on one of the most magnificent spectacles that a human being has ever beheld.

Sunrise on the moon!

To one who has not seen this incomparable sight with his own eyes no verbal description can convey a clear idea of the splendor of the lunar dawn.

Long before the uppermost edge of the sun's disc came into view, its advent was heralded by gorgeously colored shafts of living flame which shot up for enormous distances into the sable and diamond mystery of the star-studded sky. This wonderful phenomenon was caused by the corona of the sun, which is visible to observers on Earth only at rare moments during a total eclipse of the sun.

Just before the edge of the sun itself appeared, a number of smaller protuberances, fantastic in shape and brilliant pink in color, shot above the horizon.

Between us and these astonishing manifestations of cosmic illumination lay the barren plain, the distant walls of our ring mountain, and the other grotesque features of the lunar landscape, wrapped in the weird spell of the clear blue earthlight.

It was several hours before the entire circumference of the sun was visible to us, yet so wonderful and so diversified was the show put on for our benefit that none of us seemed to tire of looking at it.

I took enough time to tear my attention away from the eastern horizon and to gaze up at the zenith, where I saw my old friend the Earth in exactly the same position as I had observed her the previous evening. At first this astonished me, but a moment's reflection told me that, since the moon always keeps the same face turned toward its mother planet, there can be very little change in the position of the Earth as seen from any particular spot on the moon. Such changes as do occur are very slight and caused by the libration or tilting of the satellite in its journey around the Earth.

After going through the usual routine of washing, shaving, and of eating breakfast, we prepared to continue our exploration of the moon's surface.

As Banning and I were getting into our space suits, I asked, "By the way, Professor, would you mind telling us why you picked this particular spot for us to spend our first night on the moon?"

To which he replied, "I am anxious to settle as soon as possible certain questions, which have been the source of a great deal of guess work and argument on the part of astronomers and selenographers. The most important one is this: Is there any vegetation or other form of life on the moon? I chose this place because the interior of the ring mountain Eratosthenes is one of the regions in which a noted astronomer claims to have detected evidence that some form of vegetable life exists."

CHAPTER THIRTEEN
Answering Puzzling Questions

WHEN a traveler is writing about a strange land—describing scenes that have never before been gazed upon by human eyes—there is perhaps a strong temptation to fabricate or at least to exaggerate. It would be easy enough—with the aid of a creative imagination—to describe the moon as covered with monstrous and preposterous vegetation and inhabited with animals—some horrible, some weird, some human-like.

But since this is nothing but a straightforward, accurate account of what we actually saw and did during our sojourn on the moon, I am compelled to chronicle that no life of such extraordinary characteristics does exist on the moon.

We learned that the changes in the color of the plain inside the ring mountain Eratosthenes, which take place as the heat of the sun warms this region, were not due to vegetation—as was erroneously deduced by one or two well known astronomers. It was caused entirely by the effect of the heat on a mineral formation, which is metallic in character, Professor Banning secured samples of this mineral which were subsequently submitted to various tests. While the metal contained in them was entirely different from any substance found on Earth, the transformation caused by heat in varying degrees of intensity might be compared to the changes in the color of a piece of iron when it is subjected to high temperatures. The only essential difference was that the minerals found on the moon went through these color changes at lower temperatures—ranging from 80 degrees to 218 degrees Fahrenheit.

In order to make certain that no plants or other forms of life existed in any part of the moon, Professor Banning explored and thoroughly investigated all of the places where changes that might have been caused by vegetation had previously been observed by astronomers. Among the regions, which we visited during this visit for this purpose, were the interior of the ring mountains Plato, Aristarchus, Grimalidi, and Alphonsus. We also flew back and forth over the Sea of Serenity, approaching close enough to the surface to observe all important details, but we did not find any evidence that either animal or vegetable life had recently existed there.

For some mysterious reason, Professor Banning seemed very much pleased when he had convinced himself indubitably that no plants or animal of any description were living on the moon.

"It's much better to begin with nothing at all than to run the risk of having to fight undesirable things," he murmured, half to himself. Just what he meant by this cryptic remark I did not know until several years later.

As time is reckoned on Earth, we spent approximately ten days in exploring the half of the moon, which is visible from the Earth. All during this time I had been impatient to see what was on the far side of the lunar sphere. Professor Banning had grudgingly consented to our making one brief trip for a short distance beyond the western boundaries of the earthward hemisphere, while that portion of the moon was illuminated by the sun. Naturally, it was not feasible to penetrate beyond the lighted parts of the opposite side, since there we had no friendly earthshine to light our way as was the case on the portions which faced the Earth.

I can only report that we discovered nothing startling or unusual. The landscape on the far side of the moon was very similar to that which is visible from the Earth. The characteristic features, such as magnificent mountains, spacious craters, abysmal clefts, and glittering rays were all duplicated on the other side of the moon.

We took a large number of photographs from the air. When pieced together, these pictures constituted an aerial map of about one-fourth of the hemisphere which is turned away from the Earth. Because of the fact that a considerable part of this half of the moon was in darkness, we were not able to map it completely.

The number of actual landings we made on the far side of the moon were limited—only five to be exact. The last of these stops came very near being the termination of our adventure.

Berglin had set the *Amundsen* down on a level stretch of desolate ground about 300 miles from the imaginary line, which marked the eastern boundaries of the moon's disc as seen from the Earth.

We were all weary and had planned to rest for several hours. From the place, which we had chosen as our camping ground, we could see the sun low in the horizon, so that neither the light nor the heat was excessively intense.

In examining our surroundings before retiring, I noticed that we were close to a peculiar formation. Our flyer was just inside the angle formed by two cracks in the ground, which met at an angle of approximately 120 degrees, I estimated this from the fact that the amount of divergence seemed to be just about the same as the angle of a regular hexagon. The most remarkable thing about these cracks was that they extended as far as the eye could reach in perfectly straight lines. When I first observed them, they were only a few inches wide. Interested as I was in this unusual feature, it did not occur to me to regard it with foreboding, or even to point it out to my companions. At that particular moment I was more interested in getting some sleep than in studying geology—or perhaps I should say "selenology."

How long I slept I do not know, but when I did awake it was with a weird feeling in my bones that something was wrong. I glanced out of the window and what I saw made me utter a yell that jolted Berglin and Banning from their slumbers with rude suddenness. Stretching away from us in almost rectilinear regularity were two ridges about three feet high. They seemed to be made of thin clay or mud which oozed forth from the bowels of the moon and piled up higher and higher as we watched.

One of the ridges extended directly under our flyer. So rapidly was it increasing in size that it had almost engulfed us before we realized what was happening. "Quick!" cried the Professor. "Turn on the rear rocket tubes. Give it all you have—full speed ahead."

Berglin responded instantly, but the glutinous material, half-fluid, half solid, already had grasped us in its tenacious embrace. Fortunately, the tail of the *Amundsen* was clear; so that we could at least make a valiant attempt to escape.

For several anxious seconds our fate hung in the balance. Starting with as much power as he dared to use, Berglin quickly accelerated until the maximum force of our powerful fuel was shooting through the rocket tubes. Under the terrific strain, the *Amundsen* shivered and groaned but held together.

Then we moved forward!

At first the movement was almost imperceptible, but nevertheless it was a motion and that was enough en-couragement for us to keep trying. Inch by inch, foot by foot, we fought our way forward until, at the end of about half an hour, we cleared the ground and hopped triumphantly into space.

"Soar around for a while. I want to study this," the Professor commanded. It was then our privilege to observe a phenomenon such as mortal eyes had never before beheld—namely the birth of a crater, or ring mountain.

From our vantage point on high we were able to see that the ridge, which had threatened to engulf us, was but a part of a gigantic formation. It then became evident to me that the cracks I had seen a few hours previous had been part of an enormous hexagon. Through these fissures, semi-fluid material from below the surface had oozed out, while at the same time the section of the surface, which was thus detached, had sunk in.

It wasn't long before the flowing clay or mud had filled in the corners so that the wall changed from a hexagonal to a circular form.

"Well," said the Professor after a while. "That settles another important question that has puzzled selenographers for some time."

"What question is that, Professor?" I asked.

"The question as to how these so-called 'craters' were formed. You can easily see now that they are not craters at all, because volcanic action has nothing to do with it."

To which I replied, "Whatever it is that forms those rings, I'd just as soon steer clear of them from now on—especially the baby ones that are just getting 'borned.'"

CHAPTER FOURTEEN
Preparing for the Homeward Journey

IN planning our itinerary, Professor Banning had set the date for our departure from the moon exactly two weeks after our arrival there. The main reason for this was that at the expiration of fourteen days the moon had moved around to the opposite side of the Earth so that it was leading its mother planet in the joint march around the sun. This enabled us to make use of the momentum of the Earth on our return journey, just as we had utilized the momentum of the moon on the first part of our trip.

The fourteen days referred to were, of course, *terrestrial* days which really amounted to only one of the moon's days as recorded from sunrise to sunset.

Our supplies of oxygen, water, food, fuel and other necessities had been calculated to suffice for an absence of two weeks—with liberal safety factors provided, of course.

During this period we succeeded in accomplishing, with surprising thoroughness, all the things that the Professor had mapped out for us. These tasks were two-fold in character: First, to answer the most important questions regarding the moon which had previously puzzled and baffled astronomers, and second, to learn as much as possible about the chemical and physical composition of the moon's surface.

So important is it for mankind to know the correct answers to the questions, which for generations have been asked about the moon, that I think it will be pertinent to summarize them here. For convenience and clarity I am using the "catechism" or question and answer format:

Q. Has the moon any atmosphere?

A. No. Scientists have known this for some time, although there have been a few who thought they could detect evidence of the existence of a very tenuous atmosphere on the moon. Our investigations showed that the moon has no atmosphere comparable to that of the Earth.

Q. Is there any water on the moon?

A. Only a very small quantity, which is in the form of vapor during the lunar day and is converted into hoarfrost at night.

Q. Is there any vegetable life on the moon?

A. Since vegetable life as we know it requires both air and moisture, it is evident that no plants such as we know on Earth can exist on the moon. We found not even the slightest vestige of plant life.

Q. Is there any animal life on the moon?

A. No, for the same reasons that vegetable life could not exist there.

Q. Is there *any* form of life on the moon?

A. No.

Q. How then, can the changes in coloring which take place as the temperature changes be accounted for?

A. We found this to be due to the physical effects of heat on certain mineral substances, corresponding to the color changes in a piece of iron when it is heated.

Q. Are the so-called "craters" on the moon volcanic in character?

A. No.

Q. How were these ring mountains formed'?

A. By clay and similar semi-fluid material oozing up to the surface through cracks formed when the moon cooled.

Q. How were the rays on the moon formed?

A. When the moon cooled from a molten state, crevasses were formed in the surface, similar to the cracks, which would be produced if a hot sphere of glass were thrust into cold water. Later, these cracks became filled with a metallic substance, which reflects the light of the sun and makes them stand out brilliantly from the rest of the moon's surface.

Q. How were the deep valleys or gorges on the moon formed?

A. They must have been formed either by comets or meteors striking the moon glancing blows.

Q: Does the hemisphere of the moon, which is not visible from the Earth, differ materially from the part that is visible?

A. The topographical features are quite similar on both sides of the moon.

I realize that there is nothing especially remarkable about the foregoing information. Most of it has been suspected by the keenest students of selenography for some time. But since this is not intended to be a bit of sensational fiction, but merely a faithful account of our explorations, I must chronicle the facts as they actually existed.

In order to find out as much as possible regarding the composition of the moon's surface, Professor Banning directed me to collect samples of soil and minerals from each of the various characteristic portions of Luna's surface. Occasionally he helped me in this work, but most of the time I did the gathering alone, while Banning busied himself at a small bench, which he had fitted up as a chemical laboratory at the rear of the *Amundsen's* cabin. Here he fussed eternally with his beakers, test tubes and crucibles. For hours on end he would work in silence, then would surprise us with an unexpected whoop of triumph or a groan of disappointment. However, he did not vouchsafe to give us any explanation of his chemical researches and neither Berglin nor myself would admit being curious enough to ask him regarding his discoveries.

On the day before the one scheduled for our departure for home, however, Professor Banning issued a singular order, which could only have been predicated on something that his chemical investigation had revealed. He directed Berglin to set the flyer down close to the spot where we had previously blasted out a portion of the giant ray about a hundred miles west of ring mountain Rheitas. Again we shot off a charge of radatomite, but this time we took the precaution of piling a large number of heavy boulders over the place to be blasted, thus preventing the fragments from being thrown far from the center of the explosion.

Following the professor's instructions, I filled all the available storage space in the *Amundsen* with chunks of the material torn from the great ray.

CHAPTER FIFTEEN
An Alarming Discovery

CAME the zero hour for our departure. Momentous as this occasion was, we hopped off as nonchalantly as if we were only going on a short trip of exploration.

On our return voyage we had planned to use the same strategy which had proved successful on our trip from the Earth to the moon.

Steadily and swiftly we climbed until the ground beneath us lost its concave appearance and assumed the form of a huge ball hanging in space. We directed our flight so as to carry our flyer along the same path the moon was traveling in its journey around the sun.

By operating the four dimensional steering apparatus, we severed the gravitational tie which bound us to the moon, and then made the hairpin turn which sent us hurtling back toward the approaching Earth.

A few moments after this maneuver was completed, I noticed off to one side of us a peculiarly shaped object drifting in space. To see anything at all in what should have been an absolutely empty void gave me such a shock that I uttered a blood-curdling yell which made my two companions jump.

"Look!" I cried. "See that object out there! It must be a meteorite or something!"

"Hardly a meteorite," Professor Banning corrected me. "It looks to me like something from our flyer. Out there, with nothing to compare it with, it's hard to tell whether it is a large body far away or a small object close to us. Let's see how it looks with the glass."

Banning picked up a field glass and trained it on the mysterious object. "I thought so!" he cried. "It's a part of something from our ship! And if I'm not mistaken, it's a piece of a four-dimensional rocket tube!"

"Let me look!" He handed me the glass and I pointed it at the mysterious object.

"You're right!" I exclaimed. "It *is* a section of our four dimensional rocket tube. It must have been broken off the tube for steering us back out of hyperspace. How do you suppose that happened?"

"It probably became cracked or weakened while we were tearing ourselves loose after getting caught in the ooze from that newly formed ring mountain," the Professor suggested. "When you turned on the other four dimensional rocket tube a moment ago it gave the ship a jolt which must have loosened the weakened part."

"Is the loss of that part likely to cause any serious consequence?" Berglin inquired.

"Serious!" I said, "I'll say it's serious. Without that tube functioning properly it's going to be impossible for us to get back into three-dimensional space. It means that we are doomed to drift around in hyperspace until our oxygen, our water, and our food give out."

Berglin seemed unwilling to accept my statement. Turning to Banning, he said, "Is that true, Professor?"

"Yes," was Banning's simple response. "It's true that we'll have to stay in hyperspace until we can get that four dimensional rocket tube repaired."

"Get it repaired?" I said in a tone, which I fear was not very respectful. "You talk as if all we have to do is phone for a plumber—preferably one with a mathematical training—to fly out here and put a new four dimensional tube on our space ship."

Fortunately my sarcastic and discourteous comment did not seem to offend the Professor. He merely gave me a tolerant smile and said, "The trouble with you, my boy, is that you give up too easily. We hear a lot about the persistency of youth but after all it seems to take a man of mature years and experience to realize the fact that, no matter how hopeless a situation my be, it pays to keep on trying to get out of it."

"Do you mean that you think we still have a chance?" I said.

"Certainly. A most excellent chance. That is, providing you have enough courage and confidence in me to do what I tell you to do," said the Professor.

"After some of the things that have happened I don't feel like bragging about my courage, but as far as confidence in you is concerned, I don't think I need to tell you that I shall always be for you as I always have been. If it's just a case of taking a chance, I'd much rather be making a try at escaping rather than sitting still waiting to die."

"That's the way to talk."

"All right. What do you want me to do?" I asked.

"The first thing to do is get into your space suit."

"Would you mind telling me just what you expect of me?" I asked.

"Of course I don't mind telling you. I want you to go outside and repair that rocket tube," was his calm reply.

"But how am I going to do that? We haven't any spare tube and we haven't the material or the tools to make a new one. As for the possibility of fastening the broken parts together, I don't see how that can be done either. In the first place we can't get hold of the broken part and in the second place it wouldn't do us any good anyway, because we haven't any welding apparatus or any other way to fasten the broken parts together."

"But how about the other four dimensional rocket tube?"

"You mean the one we employed to shoot us into hyperspace with?"

"Yes. We don't need that any more, do we?"

"I suppose not. All that can do is get us further into hyperspace. What we need is something to get us away from hyperspace."

"Exactly. Except that they pointed in opposite directions, the two four-dimensional rocket tubes were identical in shape and structure, were they not?"

"Of course."

"Then all we have to do is remove the good rocket tube and bolt it on the place where the broken tube was; then we'll be able to navigate back into three dimensional space."

"The way you describe it, the job is as simple as changing a tire on an automobile," I remarked as I began getting into the space suit.

"You may find it even easier than that," was the Professor's reply.

"Oh well, I suppose somebody has to do it. So here goes."

"You won't require all those tools," said Banning, pointing to the trowel and pickaxe which hung at my belt. "You may need the hammer, though, and of course the monkey wrench will be the most useful of all. Let me suggest, though, that you fill those empty pockets with chunks of this material that we blasted from the great ray on the moon."

"What's the idea? Am I supposed to play a cosmic game of duck on the rock, or something like that?"

"Never mind the wisecracks. The lumps of rock will make you heavier and they may come in handy for another purpose." With that he opened the door of the airlock and started to screw on my helmet.

"Just a minute!" I shouted. "You're not trying to get rid of me, are you?"

"Of course not. We may need you to do some more stunts before we get back home. Why did you ask such a question?" he asked.

"How fast are we going now?"

"About 66,000 miles per hour."

"Whew! How do you expect me to hang on to the ship when it's going at such a speed? I'll be blown to smithereens the minute I stick my nose outside!" I cried.

"Nothing of the sort. Don't you realize that your body is moving with the same velocity as the flyer and in the same direction? Relatively speaking, the *Amundsen* will be standing still so far as you are concerned. You must remember that out here there is no air or other gas to offer any resistance or to form a draft."

"But suppose I should slip and fall off the flyer?"

"There's no danger of that, either. You can't fall away from the flyer unless something pushes you or pulls you. We are in hyperspace now and neither the moon, the Earth, nor any other body is exerting any appreciable attraction for the flyer or for your body. On the other hand, there is a small but none the less potent gravitational attraction between your body and the space ship, so the only way you are likely to fall is toward the *Amundsen.*"

Satisfied at last, I entered the airlock, sealed the inner door and turned on the valve to remove the air from the small chamber. But despite Banning's optimistic assurances, there was a feeling of trepidation in my heart when I opened the outer door.

In my earphones I heard Banning's voice say, "Can you hear me?"

"Sure!" I radioed back to him. "Your program is coming in fine. Suppose you put on the record and play 'Happy Days Are Here Again.'"

"Perhaps it will be more appropriate if I play 'Get Out and Get Under the Moon!'" was his comeback.

"Well, here goes nothing!" I shouted as I eased my inflated form through the narrow opening.

Much as I depended on the correctness of Professor Banning's statements, I was astonished to discover that the flyer did seem to be floating motionless in space. With my mechanical hand I kept a tight grip on the handle of the door. There seemed to be no strain on my arm. By way of experiment I released my hold, but kept on the alert so I could make a quick grab for the handle in case I needed to. Instead of dropping or being blown away, my body swayed gently toward the flyer.

With the instinctive idea of getting on the part of the ship, which we called the top, I started to pull myself up the side of the flyer. I found to my surprise that it was just as easy to stay on the bottom as on any other part of the craft. I tried crawling completely around the ship and had the peculiar sensation that I was on top all the time, while the *Amundsen* seemed to spin beneath me, as a barrel turns when a circus performer balances himself on it.

CHAPTER SIXTEEN
Man Overboard!

I WORKED my way around to the broken rocket. It took me but a few minutes to unscrew the six nuts, which held the stump in place. Placing the nuts in a pocket, which I had kept empty for that purpose I removed the damaged tube and let go of it, I expected it to drop out of sight, but instead it clung to the side of the flyer.

In a similar manner I removed the good four-dimensional tube, but took good care not to let go of it. The only difficulty I encountered in fastening the tube in place at the other opening was that the broken fragment, which I had just removed, kept bumping against my helmet.

Working as I was under a severe nervous strain, it was exasperating to have this lump of metal banging against me, but I didn't do anything about it until I had screwed the last nut home. Then I grabbed the offending object in my mechanical fist and heaved it away from me with all my might.

To say that what happened next surprised me would be putting it mildly. Before I realized it, I found myself shooting away from the *Amundsen* at an alarming rate of speed. By the time I recovered myself enough to yell for help, I was probably at least a mile away from the space flyer, with the gap between us widening constantly.

If you can imagine how it would feel to fall off an ocean liner in mid-ocean, you will have a faint idea of how I felt as I drifted out there in that awful void and watched the space ship grow smaller and smaller in the distance.

The worst of it was that neither Banning nor Berglin seemed to have noticed my departure, since I had been working near the tail of the flyer where they could not see me through the windows.

Finally, I gained command of my vocal chords and yelled, "Help! Help! Man overboard!"

Instantly, the welcome voice of the Professor came to me through the earphones: "How in the world did you get way out there?"

"Search me. It happened right after I threw away the broken rocket tube."

"You threw it away? That accounts for it. The reaction from the force of the tube as it left your hand pushed you in the opposite direction."

"I suppose you are going to tell me that I'm suffering from the effects of one of Newton's laws of motion. But right now I'm more interested in getting back to the ship. Can't you swing around here and pick me up before I get any further away?"

"That would be a dangerous thing to attempt, I'm afraid. If we should turn on any of the rocket tubes at the speed we are traveling, it is likely to alter our momentum so much that you'd never be able to hang on, even if we could come close enough for you to reach us."

"Do you mean to tell me that there is no hope for me— that I'm doomed to hang out here forever?"

"Of course there's hope for you. If you'll just keep your head and do as I say, you'll be back here in a few minutes. It would be risky for us to try to come to you, but that doesn't prevent you from coming back to us."

"What do you want me to do, swim back? When it comes to swimming in this stuff, I'm afraid my training has been sadly neglected. I'll do my best, though," and I started kicking with my legs and waving my arms.

"That won't do you any good," the Professor told me. "Better save your strength. The best way to get back here is to use the same principle that sent you out there."

"What do you mean?"

"The force of reaction. Your pockets are full of rocks. Suppose you get one of them in your mechanical hand, then take careful sight toward the flyer and throw the missile in exactly the opposite direction. This will make you move toward us."

I followed his instructions and sure enough I began to move slowly in the general direction of the *Amundsen*. To accelerate my speed, I hurled two more rocks. My aim was fair but far from perfect, I was still at least a hundred feet away from the ship as I swept past it and beyond it.

This got me excited and I started heaving my missiles with all my might in rapid succession. In this manner I succeeded in projecting myself directly at the space ship, but when I reached it, my speed was so great that I had no time to grab hold of anything. Like a huge rubber ball, my inflated space suit bumped into the side of the flyer and bounced briskly away again.

"Keep your head!" the Professor warned me. "Take time to aim carefully and try to judge your speed more accurately."

"What do you think this is," I retorted, "a cosmic golf game? If I slice my shots I get in the rough, and if I hit 'em too hard I bounce off the green, I'm afraid I'll never make par on this hole, but here goes for another try."

Perhaps I shouldn't have made this feeble attempt to be funny if I had realized that my ammunition was running short. I was still several feet away from the *Amundsen* when I discovered to my horror that my last chunk of lunar rock was gone. I was about to give up in despair when I happened to think of the six extra nuts which I had taken from the broken rocket tube.

"Thank Heaven I saved them," I said to myself.

After that there was no more fooling—no more prodigal waste of my precious missiles. With all the care of an expert playing in a championship match, I tossed the first of the nuts. It brought me closer, but a trifle to one side of my target. This I corrected by carefully throwing the second nut, I still had one of the metal objects left when I finally nudged gently against the side of the space ship and caught hold of a strut. Naturally I lost no time in getting inside the airlock and closing the door behind me.

CHAPTER SEVENTEEN
Back to Earth

THE remainder of our journey was uneventful. When the proper moment arrived, Professor Banning instructed me to direct a blast through the four dimensional rocket tube. It worked perfectly, bringing us back into the influence of the Earth's gravitational attraction.

In returning, we duplicated the same maneuver we had used in landing on the moon; that is we made a hairpin turn, around the Earth, so that we were traveling in the same direction and at about the same speed as our planet was moving in its orbit. Then, with the aid of our rocket motors, we sped through the upper regions of the Earth's atmosphere until we could make out the topographical features of the land beneath us.

Under the skillful guidance of Berglin, we navigated our craft until we were hovering over our home field at San Diego. Here a most alarming sight met our gaze. As far as the eye could perceive, the roads in all directions were jammed solid with automobiles, motorcycles, and other conveyances. Out in San Diego Harbor there was an inconceivable jumble of boats of all kinds and sizes, from canoes to battleships. So close were they packed that a person could have walked from San Diego to Coronado, on the opposite shore, merely by climbing from one boat to another.

The air was so thick with airplanes that we had difficulty in keeping out of their way. Worst of all, the field on which we were expected to land was packed full with a surging, milling mass of humanity.

It looked as if all California with additional representatives from Arizona and Old Mexico, had gathered in that one spot to greet us. To attempt a landing under such circumstances was out of the question.

"Let's go to Clover Field," Berglin suggested, and Banning agreed.

The enormous swarm of airplanes attempted to follow us, but so swiftly did our rocket motors carry us that we soon left them far behind. We found the field at Santa Monica absolutely deserted. Not an airplane, not a human being was in evidence. Apparently they had all gone to meet us at San Diego.

"In a way this is very fortunate for us," Professor Banning said. "It will give us a chance to unload our cargo without having a lot of curious reporters snooping around. There are very strong reasons why I don't want anybody to know what we brought back with us from the moon."

"Would you mind letting Berglin and me know what this stuff is?" I asked. "You know of course that you can depend on us to keep it under our hats."

"Why of course you are entitled to know. It is platinum—pure, unadulterated platinum."

"And how much is it worth?"

"About one hundred and ten dollars per ounce."

"One hundred and ten dollars per what?"

"One hundred and ten dollars per ounce. But the monetary worth of platinum is not so important as its value in science and industry. As you probably know, there are a number of cases where platinum has to be used in spite of its high cost. In some chemical operations, for instance, platinum receptacles must be used. Another illustration is in dentistry. One reason why porcelain jacketed crowns are so expensive is that they are made over a platinum shell. In many ways a dependable supply of cheap platinum would be of great advantage to humanity."

"Well, now that we have all this platinum here, what are we going to do with it?" I asked.

"That looks like an ideal hiding place," the Professor replied as he pointed to a ramshackle building just across the road from the airport. It had formerly been used as a real estate office. With the selling out of the subdivision, the building had apparently been abandoned by had been left standing. Its ruinous appearance made it only the safer for our purpose.

"We'd better hurry," Banning admonished us. "It won't be long before that flock of airplanes will arrive from San Diego."

Between the three of us, we carried the chunks of metal to the building, piling the material in such a way that it could not be seen through the windows.

"Some dark night, we'll come out here with a truck and remove the platinum," Banning observed, as he closed the door of the building.

Just then something struck my funny bone and I started to laugh.

"What's the matter with our facetious friend now?" the Professor inquired.

"I just had a mental picture of myself out there in space, heaving away lumps of platinum worth a thousand dollars apiece, as if they were mere pebbles."

"Don't worry about that," said Professor Banning. "There's plenty more where that platinum came from— thousands of tons of it!"

THE END